"What do you suppose *would* have happened in the bedroom?" David asked darkly

They both knew what would have happened on that bedroom floor. Gina never could resist him. Weak! Weak and stupid, that's what she was! "Nothing would have happened!" It was a bitter lie, but she couldn't deal with the truth. In self-defense, she embellished on the lie. "I'm over you, David. You're inflexible and manipulative. Why can't you go back to Boston?" She banged the spatula on the kitchen countertop.

"Because I'm inflexible and manipulative." He got that knowing look in his eyes again. "Gina . . ."

"What!" she cried out. "What momentous, earth-shattering revelation must you relate to me now? I doubt if I can go on one more instant without yet another brilliant insight from you. Go ahead! Dazzle me!"

"I just thought you should know," he began, smiling sardonically, "that the grease in the pan is on fire."

Renee Roszel loves dominant, intelligent men, and she married a man like that. In *Unwilling Wife*, Renee's hero is everything a woman could want— except for a well-meaning tendency toward tyranny. With her heroine, Renee dealt with many of the same dilemmas she's faced in her own marriage. *Unwilling Wife* is a rollicking romp through one determined woman's attempt to teach her man a thing or two about fair play in a relationship. And her hero, like Renee's husband, is such a dear, that it's worth the effort. Look for Renee's first Harlequin Romance novel, *Prince of Delights*, in May 1992.

Books by Renee Roszel
HARLEQUIN TEMPTATION
246—ANOTHER HEAVEN
279—LEGENDARY LOVER
334—VALENTINE'S KNIGHT

Unwilling Wife

RENEE ROSZEL

Harlequin Books

TORONTO • NEW YORK • LONDON
AMSTERDAM • PARIS • SYDNEY • HAMBURG
STOCKHOLM • ATHENS • TOKYO • MILAN

For the daughters in the world
who lost their dads too soon:
To us
And to them;
Most especially,
To
Norman V. Roszel

Published January 1992

ISBN 0-373-25478-4

UNWILLING WIFE

1

GINA WAS OUT OF BREATH and close to tears, but she forced herself to keep her mind on the business at hand—getting rid of The Dean's Wife! With gritty determination, she dragged the bulging suitcase down the stone steps from the lighthouse to the foam-scalloped beach.

The bonfire she'd built was blazing. With the dying sun aflame far out on the heaving Pacific, the whole world, it seemed, was eerily drenched in crimson, taking on a bright foreboding—as though there was something dreadfully wrong with the air, the sea and the pink-hued sand. Gina bit her trembling lips. This was no time for faltering. She'd made her decision. Just because the raging fire of the dying day gave off an impression of widespread carnage, that was no reason to conjure up ill omens.

She inhaled deeply, reviving herself with the crisp, salt-laden air. Gina was about to declare herself, once and for all, a separate and equal person—devoid of any further entanglement with the patronizing, dictatorial David Baron!

Her resolve strengthened, she flipped open the suitcase fasteners, recalling the time David had brought it home, so delighted with his gift for her. It was a beautiful, monogrammed piece of leather luggage, but it had been his choice, not hers. She'd wanted the cute plaid set, but he'd said the fabric wouldn't wear well, and that she would soon tire of the busy design.

"Well, we'll never know now," she muttered aloud, as she dragged out an armful of her clothes and flung them into the middle of the greedy flames. "Goodbye you ugly aqua-chiffon formal! Last year at the Professors' Wives' Association installation of officers, when I was required to wear you, I looked like a fat glob of cotton candy and smelled of mothballs. *Never again!* And goodbye you homely, hand-tatted dickies—annual Christmas punishment from our college president's dull wife! And so long, you squatty pillbox hat, stupid white gloves, and *you*, especially—you horrid black wool commencement suit!

"Get lost, you wimpy Pep Club beanie!" With an angry flip of her wrist, she hurled a discus-shaped object into the flames, declaring, "May I be devoured by hungry bears before I ever again have to utter the phrase, 'Scramble, Iguanas, Scramble'!"

Another hearty toss disposed of her purple jersey floor-length VIP Reception dress. "Goodbye and good riddance to all of you, and to the Dean's correct little wife!" she muttered.

A twig snapped from somewhere in the shadows behind her—the unmistakable sound of someone approaching. Having just picked up another shoe, Gina spun toward the sound, her arm raised, prepared to defend herself as one can when armed with nothing more than a sling-back, summer pump. "Who's there?" she cried in a fearful whisper.

Sweetheart Point's lighthouse, a gingerbread cottage, painted yellow and trimmed in white, with its tower striped yellow and white like a giant candy stick, was located on an isolated spine of land. It was perched on a craggy cliff facing an expansive vista of ocean, just fifty yards from a cathedral-like setting of redwoods and cypress trees that masked the secluded retreat from the access road. Its beach was out-of-the-way and remote, ten miles from the nearest neighbor. No one should be wandering about. Sinister possibilities flooded her brain, and she shivered.

She searched the shadow for signs of life hidden in the blackness of the towering rock wall. Then she saw it—tall, wide shouldered, a menacing specter, especially for a woman alone with nothing but a flimsy shoe as defense. "Who's there?" she repeated, willing her voice to be strong, unafraid.

He took a step forward, and she flinched at the stab of recognition she felt in the pit of her stomach. But, no, it wouldn't be, couldn't be—

"While you're destroying things, darling—" a masculine voice cut through her musings "—why don't we destroy these?"

Horror swept through her. The deep, sardonic voice could belong to no one but her soon-to-be ex-husband. Yet, it simply couldn't be David. She'd left him a month and three thousand miles ago.

"It can't be—you. . . ." she gasped filled with dismay.

"No? Who were you expecting, my love?" he returned bitterly.

Gina had grown deathly still, but her heart thumped uncontrollably as his imposing form emerged from the ruddy dusk into the fire's burnished glow. Precisely dressed, darkly handsome, he could be no one else but—

"David," she whispered, lowering her arm in a state of complete shock. Still, she retained the presence of mind to clutch the shoe like a weapon. He looked as if he might be capable of any violent act right now. Fearful, she asked, "What are you doing here?"

"I've already told you," he retorted. "I brought something to burn." He circled around her in that sedate yet sexy saunter that had always turned her to mush, and, even now, she found she had to steel herself against it. Lean and broad-shouldered, his silhouette appeared even more striking than she recalled as he moved between her and the fire.

She watched his stalwart profile, hardened in anger, as he neared the fiery beast that was ravenously consuming the physical evidence of the ten years of their life together. He was holding what looked like a batch of papers. With infuriated dispatch he tossed them into the flames. This done, he turned to confront her. His face was half lit by the fire, his brown hair, glowing a rich mahogany color, as he vowed, "There will be no divorce between us, Gina. Not while I live."

She forced herself to face his hardened stare. "It's done, David," she protested hotly. "Face it and go back to Boston."

"Like hell, sweetheart."

His tone was cold, his features twisted with hurt and rage. His lips were drawn down in a thin-lined scowl— those full, masculine lips that had seemed to be made for smiling. She realized she'd hardly ever seen David angry. Of course, that was because David had always made the decisions. *Gina, darling, your hair looks so much neater pulled back away from your face. Gina, my love, you will never forgive yourself if you don't volunteer for the campus beautification committee. Gina, for your own good, you should reconsider taking up bowling. You'd be much wiser to enroll in aerobics. Gina, as the dean of the physics department's wife, you'll be expected to entertain, so I've signed you up for a gourmet cooking class.* And on, and on it had gone! Ten years of dominating and controlling, instructing and cajoling with a smile and a kiss.

Well, now, for once, when things weren't going his way, he was madder than she'd ever imagined he could be; he'd taken on the look of a wounded beast. His gray eyes, shadowed by wicked, curling lashes, glittered severely.

"What did you throw on the fire?" she managed, her voice tight.

He smiled—a grim show of teeth that made her blanch. "Our divorce papers, darling. What did you *think* I'd do with them? Frame them and hang them in the den?"

"Our divorce..." she echoed, her fears confirmed. "You can't just burn them!"

"Like, hell, I can't. That's where they belong." He moved a step toward her. "Do you have any idea where I was when those blasted documents were delivered to me?"

Unable to withstand his intent gaze, she scanned the blood-red foam of the darkening sea, and struggled to appear unaffected. "How could I know that?"

"I'll tell you, then. I was guest-lecturing at Harvard. That smirking baboon of a sheriff's officer bounded up to the podium and thrust them under my nose in the middle of my 'Wonderful World of Waves' speech."

She pictured him—so correct, so conservative, so respectable—standing there before hundreds of students and faculty. Interrupted in mid-oration, he lost his renowned cool and became downright flustered upon discovering his wife wanted out of their marriage. She was positive he'd been more mortified than most people would be caught nude in the middle of a busy intersection. Feeling a surge of delicious glee, she chided, "It looks as though I've finally made a few waves in your wonderful world!"

His expression menacing, he took another step toward her.

Gina backed away. When she did, she saw distress flash across his face.

"Damn it, Gina," he protested. "Do you really think I'd hurt you?"

She stared at him for a long moment as his eyes searched her face, his expression furious yet somehow vulnerable. She shook her head. "No—you wouldn't hurt me, David."

"What in heaven's name is all this about?" he asked, this time without malice. "I thought, after giving you a month to come out here to think things over, you'd come home. But yesterday, when those damned papers were delivered to me, I couldn't believe it."

She should have known David wouldn't simply sign them and fade silently out of her life, and that he'd come after her. He wasn't the type to simply fade away.

That day, ten years ago, when he'd first walked into the bookshop her father had just bought, she'd known it immediately. He was a man who knew what he wanted and got it. She'd been nineteen, and it was her first day behind the counter when the tall, striking college professor had ambled up to her, graced her with a heart-stopping grin and said, "Working here, you must love books."

She'd been nonplused, telling him her father had owned a sporting-goods store for the past five years, and that the book business was new to her. He simply continued to smile, promising, "You'll learn to love them. I'll teach you." Then he'd told her he would be back at six o'clock to pick her up for dinner—not even knowing her name. She'd been thrilled by his take-charge personality. He'd been a self-possessed, secure man, like her father, and she'd been drawn to him instantly.

So bold, so sure of himself, so determined to get his way, David had remained the same. But as she'd matured, his desire to nurture and teach her had grown tedious and restrictive. And when her mother had died... She shook off the unhappy memory. Well, she'd promised herself things would change. She couldn't allow his domination over her to continue. Her whole future depended on her being strong—*now*. Still, she'd been hopelessly naive to think he would give her up without a fight.

Not sure how to handle this, she resumed feeding the fire. Stooping down, she tossed another load of clothes onto the flames. This time she noticed a red knit dress fly into the inferno and pointed to it with a jerky wave of her hand. "There. I hope that makes you happy. Since *you* bought that dress for me, I thought it would be permissible to wear it to the college president's house. Silly me, for not asking for detailed wearing instructions! Well, I won't be embarrassing you at any more college functions, turning up in inappropriate clothes!"

David's brow knit in consternation as he watched the dress blacken and disintegrate into ash and smoke. "Dammit, Gina, all this can't be because of that! Besides, it was you—my loving wife of ten years—who dumped a serving platter of aspic over my head in front of the entire Albert Einstein faculty." Frustration tinged his voice. "Who do you thing was humiliated? You, when I whispered that you might consider wearing something less snug to the college president's home, or me, when you tossed that glutinous mess over my head and ran out wailing. If you'll recall, sweetheart, that party was in my honor." His tone grew caustic. "What kind of time do you think I had once you were gone and I was left there—alone—with tomato aspic dripping down my face?"

She sighed heavily, not wanting to think about it. That had been a terrible thing to do to him, but it had been the last straw in ten years of straws! It should have been a happy occasion—a party celebrating the critical acclaim he'd received for his latest physics textbook. But his condescending remark about her dress had been the final blow, and she'd gone a little crazy.

Trying to control her raw emotions with physical activity, she lugged the now empty suitcase to the fire and threw it on the crackling heap. When she'd competed her final act of defiance, she turned to face David. Observing his pained expression as he watched his most recent gift to her scorch and shrivel before his eyes, she felt grimly victorious.

"David," she began, breathless from exertion and tenseness, "I suppose I shouldn't have done that—I mean the thing with the aspic. But you *never* listened to me. Every time I told you I wanted to do something that deviated—even slightly—from your *idea* of what was proper, you patted me on the head, kissed me, made me do it your way and told me I'd thank you for it later. Remember that community-theater production of *Hair* I got a part in, and you made me drop out?"

"It was impossible for me to allow you to go naked onstage!" he protested.

"Impossible for *you!*" she spat. "The director told us we could perform undressed or not—according to our moral standards. I don't know what I would have done, David. The point is, you didn't allow me to make that decision."

"But, darling, I'm a college dean. There are standards—"

"I know all about your standards! And, I *don't* thank you for your concerned attempts to instill them in me. I'm tired of being married to a man who treats me like a mindless Kewpi doll!"

"That's absurd. I think of you in no such way. Is it too much to ask that a man's wife show a little decorum?"

"Is it too much to ask that a husband show his wife a little faith?"

He scowled. "All I ask is that you be concerned with my well-being, my wants and needs. Isn't that what all men want?"

"You want a sex slave! And maybe some men do want that—if they're macho jerks."

"You're being melodramatic," he admonished softly. "I merely want to be proud of you, to display you as my charming life's companion—"

"Like a prize hog!" she broke in.

"No, of course not. Don't you understand, I want you well versed in the correct way of the running of a household and the elegant entertaining of our colleagues—"

"*Dammit*, David! What you want is a submissive, sex-starved charwoman who can win you blue ribbons at the state fair!" she cried, effectively cutting him off. She'd had this fight bottled up inside her for a long time, and having David show up when she'd quit vacillating—finally having decided to make radical changes in her life—was like putting dynamite to a dam. The floodwaters of her discontent came gushing out in a torrent of harsh words.

"I have no intention of being a submissive, sex-starved charwoman with a chest full of blue ribbons for you—not anymore!" she retorted. "Just because you're thirteen years older than I am, and just because I married you when I was nineteen and you were a high-and-mighty physics professor, doesn't mean you can go on acting like my father—my master—forever. I'm a grown woman! I need to be given a chance to do my own thing—to spread my wings and fly! My way!"

"I think I understand." He nodded reluctantly, his expression softening. "You're upset because you're going to turn thirty next month. Gina, darling," he offered more gently, "lots of women face their own mortality when they're about to—"

"No!" She stomped her bare foot. "This has nothing to do with turning thirty or mortality! This is about my wholeness! The me I want to be! I've outgrown you, David. It first hit me when mother was dying...." Unable to go on, she bit her lip to regain her composure.

"Your mother?" he asked. "She died five years ago. What could that possibly have to do with us, now?"

"Everything! Don't you see? When Dad died, Mother just faded away. As she lay dying, she told me how alike she and I were—how devoted I was to being your wife. How proud she was of me. And she smiled, David. She actually smiled. She was dying because she was nothing but an empty shell after my father died, and she didn't even see that as a tragedy." Gina's voice broke and she struck away a tear angrily. "I've tried, David. I've tried to tell you for five years. I'm through trying! I refuse to be dissolved bodily into your life force. And that's what will happen to me if I stay with you. You're so strong, so dominant, and every day I can feel myself slipping further and further away from the person I want to be. I—I want to be somebody in my own right—not just the dean of the physic's department's ... *wifely tentacle*."

He scowled. "You're being hysterical. No one could every consider you any such disgusting thing. But you're damn well going to remain my wife, because I have no intention of letting you go."

"You'll have to, because I've moved out here to Northern California for good. This lighthouse was left to me by Grandpa Johnson, and I intend to make a new life for myself here."

"In a deserted lighthouse?" His voice had grown incredulous.

She nodded. "I realize it is rather unorthodox by your standards. But I can't be bothered by what you approve of or disapprove of, anymore." His heated gaze seemed to dare her to go on. With a trace of reservation, she took that dare. "I—I'm here. I intend to stay. And it's none of your business."

In the flickering firelight, she was witness to a twisted mockery in his smile. "You're wrong, darling," he corrected, his tone threatening, his eyes glittering like coals. "It's just as much my business as it is yours."

She frowned, feeling a shiver of unease creep up her spine. "What do you mean?"

In three strides he was upon her, looming over her, close—so close she could detect his musky, erotic scent. Refusing to be cowed by this obvious attempt at intimidation or by his disturbing masculinity, she stood her ground, repeating tightly, "What do you mean?"

"I mean," he ground out, "that according to California community-property laws, anything you inherited during our marriage automatically becomes half mine."

He paused, allowing the truth of his statement to soak in, watching until her eyes were wide with understanding. His tone chilly and definite, he finished, "I, my love, am moving into *our* lighthouse with you."

She heard her breath catch, felt her heartbeat quicken. "No . . . never . . ."

"I knew you'd be pleased," he observed dryly.

"You're lying," she shot back, alarmed. David wasn't one to make idle threats or to play games. He was a man who got the facts and used them to his advantage. With a sinking feeling that he knew something she didn't, she found herself close to pleading. "You—you are lying, David. I won't allow this. I won't allow you to manipulate me—not anymore." She flung an arm up toward the rocky cliff where the windows of her lighthouse haven glowed golden in the darkness. "Just haul your carcass back up there and get out of here the same way you came, because I'm not going to put up with any last-ditch—"

"Save your breath," he cut across her words, as an envelope materialized in his hand. "I had that ass of a lawyer you hired write this, because I knew you'd only believe it from him. He may be a low, crawling snake, but at least he can spell out the law quite clearly." David handed the letter to her, or rather, placed it in her hand. She wasn't able to move, she was so stunned. When she said nothing, he went on, "Feel free to read it by the firelight. And when you've finished your adolescent display of temper, why don't you join me inside?"

Crushing the damnable letter in shaky fingers helped her find her voice, and she sputtered, "I—won't!"

He arched an eyebrow as though it were immaterial to him. "Fine. You can spend the night on the beach."

Her mouth worked in bewilderment before she finally shouted, "I—I won't be put out of my own home!"

"I wouldn't think of doing such a thing." His lips lifted in a cold, sardonic grin. Gina had never seen such an unprincipled look before—especially on the handsome features of her starched, scholarly husband. He went on, almost benevolently, "You're perfectly welcome—any time."

He turned away, leaving her to stare dumbly after him. As he took on the hundred-foot incline of stone steps, two at a time, she tugged her stricken gaze from his receding form and looked down at the crumpled letter in her hand. Recognizing her lawyer's letterhead, she dejectedly unfolded it and read the awful truth: David hadn't been lying. As usual, he had things well under control. With a feeling of hopelessness enveloping her, she moaned, "This can't be happening to me!"

Sweetheart Point's beach had seemed a made-to-order sanctuary, and Gina had fallen in love with its peace and solitude. But right now, she felt invaded. The isolated world where she'd planned to heal and begin again had suddenly become a battleground, with the enemy, at this very minute, occupying her territory like a tyrannical dictator! As she trudged up the meandering, rough-hewn steps, she grew more and more outraged by David's domineering tactics!

How dare he come here and demand to take up residence with her! By the time she'd reached the white picket fence that separated the rocky cliff from her carefully tended front yard and her pink-blossomed azaleas, she was ready to commit mayhem. Slamming into the bungalow, she almost ran into him.

"Well, well," he chided easily, looking all too smug. "I see you've decided to join me."

"Listen," she said, jabbing at his chest with her forefinger. "I may not have the strength or even the legal right to toss you out on your erudite backside, but if you insist on staying here, then there are going to be rules."

He quirked an eye, looking insufferably amused. Apparently, once he'd set foot inside her domain, his attitude had lightened measurably. He'd probably decided he could coax her back with reason and logic—wear her down, demonstrate to her the rightness of it, as he usually did. Well, not this time!

"What rules, darling?"

"And that's another thing," she returned hotly. "Quit calling me that. I'm not your 'darling.'"

"It's not a habit I intend to abandon," he advised smoothly.

She moaned, eyeing the beamed ceiling. "You're going to drive me crazy!"

"No, Gina," he corrected her, his tone resolute. "Just back into my arms."

She shot him a sharp glance. "I'm going to ignore that." Stalking to the kitchen, she burrowed around in a drawer, tossing odd, unrecognizable things out and cursing freely under her breath. After a time, she came up with what she'd been looking for—a roll of electrician's tape.

David eyed her curiously. "What are you doing?"

She turned a cunning glance at him, but said nothing. Marching past him, she yanked at the ragged end of the tape, dropped to her knees before the door that led to the lighthouse tower, and began to divide the room down the middle, crawling backward slowly, pressing the tape down as she went.

"That's very inventive, Gina," David drawled. "But the rug doesn't look like it needs fixing."

She bumped into something and turned around. David was standing there, every inch the enlightened Yuppie, in his hand-knit cardigan, button-down shirt, classic gabardine slacks—even down to his shiny tassel moccasins. It had been one of those shoes she'd backed into as he stood there, long legs planted on either side of her.

"Will you *please* move!" It had more the sound of a curse than a request.

"What are you doing?" he asked, skepticism ripe in his tone, though it was clear to Gina that he already had a fairly good idea.

Sitting back on her haunches, she scowled up at him. "I'm dividing the house—half for you, half for me. And I don't want you to touch anything on my side! Is that clear, Professor?"

He eyed her with doubt. "If you'll notice, the front door is on one side and the bedroom and bath are on the other. There may have to be a few compromises."

She laughed out loud at that. "You? Compromise? That'll be cute."

When she'd turned back to her work, she muttered a spate of words, three of which David could understand. He gritted his teeth. The woman that he would give up his life for had just called him a "bullying, pigheaded jerk." Things weren't working out exactly as he'd hoped. He'd fantasized that Gina would run into his arms the moment she saw him. So much for that fantasy! If it didn't promise to hurt so much, he could almost laugh.

David found himself caught in a trap. Dammit! He loved her so much! Didn't she know that everything he'd done, he'd done for her? Why the hell was she so mad? He'd only been trying to help when he'd told her how to wear her hair or to give up her penchant for chocolate sodas. All he'd ever wanted to do was show her affection. Was it so damnably bad that he'd improved her wardrobe and her diet in the process?

He'd lived in fancy boarding schools in England since he was ten years old. His dad had been dominating, his mother submissive. That kind of behavior was all he knew. He'd been glad to leave a home where there hadn't been much love, and though the boarding school had been strict, he'd flourished there, because his instructors had rewarded his efforts. He'd grown up to emulate his beloved teachers—learning to show love by offering guidance. That's why, even having inherited a fortune, he'd chosen to be a college professor. He cared about young people and wanted to enrich their lives as his teachers and mentors had enriched his.

But now, the one person in the world he loved beyond all else, wanted to rid herself of him, as though he were an old, worn-out overcoat. He wondered if she'd ever realized he'd tried to keep himself in shape for her. Being thirteen years her senior, he'd hoped all the things he'd done for her would bind her to him so closely that she would never want a younger man; would never regret her decision to marry him. He'd worried about their age difference for years, and because of it, he'd tried to become indispensable to her so she wouldn't turn to someone else; but now, it seemed that maybe his efforts had been in vain.

It killed his soul to know that he'd lost Gina's love—that, in her own, devastating words she'd "outgrown him." But he wouldn't let that defeat him! He had no idea what to do to get her back. He'd been hurt and confused when she'd walked out, but once he'd been served those cursed papers—well, *enough was enough!* For her own good, he'd put a stop to this defiant foolishness of hers. Though he was in too damned much pain to have a good handle on exactly what he was going to do to get her back, he was here. They were together; and that was a beginning.

"I said, move!" she repeated, nudging his rock-hard calf with her elbow. "David, I hope you don't think brute force is going to help."

He swallowed the angry bile that blocked his throat and made do with a careworn frown. "I'm sorry dar—Gina, but I don't know whàt side I'm supposed to take."

She was startled by his sudden capitulation. "Oh—er..." She decided to give him the side with the couch and the front door, leaving her the bedroom. She waved him that way. "Of course, you'll have to allow me a path to the door."

He inclined his head agreeably, but his frown remained intact. "Of course."

That was easy enough, Gina thought, feeling a rush of satisfaction.

"And which side of the bed would you have me take?"

Her gaze sped to his face. "The bedroom's on my side," she explained, fresh suspicion in her tone.

He shrugged his hands into his pockets. "But half the bed is mine."

"Who says!"

"California's community-property laws."

Gina groaned. "Okay, then you take that side. I'll take the couch."

He stepped back across the makeshift dividing line before turning to face her again. "Gina, have you forgotten your bicycling accident? With those two fused vertebrae, you have to sleep on a hard bed."

She dropped her gaze, taking up her backward scooting along the scratchy rug. Smoothing down the tape as she went, she muttered, "My bad back is no longer your business. The couch will be just fine."

"But, sweet—"

"*Don't!*" she interrupted, shifting so that he could see the determination on her face. "David. I'm not sleeping with you, and that's final!"

His eyes were strangely luminous in the lamplight. "Are you afraid?" he asked.

She blanched. Why did the mention of sharing a bed with him make her feel so defensive? "No! I'm not afraid. How ridiculous," she lied. "Can't you understand that I just don't want you around?"

She backed onto the kitchen's linoleum tiles, the floor suddenly cold against her bare knees. David didn't say anything else, and she didn't look up to see where he was. When she reached the end of the narrow room, she ran into a table leg. Unrolling the tape with a loud z-i-i-i-i-p, she stood and divided the tabletop in half, finally stopping the division where the table butted up against the window.

"David, you may use half of my divided sink if I may use two of your stove burners."

"This is crazy," he groused. "Of course, you may use two of my burners. Damn it, Gina how long are we going to play this child's game?"

She spun to face him as he leaned against the kitchen door, his tall frame filling the open space. "Until you give up and go home," she vowed quietly.

"I have no home without you," he retorted, his tone bitter.

She felt the stab of his words, heard the hurt in them, but fought the urge to be affected. Tossing him a contemptuous glare, she flattened herself against the door frame to avoid his touch, and made a brisk exit from the kitchen. "I don't have time to stand around and chat. I have things to do."

"Have you eaten?"

"Don't worry about me. You're not my mother." She started to cross the line to get to the bedroom, but looked back at him for a minute, about to ask his permission, but she caught herself. With a haughty sniff, she stalked across his space and disappeared into the bedroom.

After a moment, she noticed that he had come to stand in the doorway. By then, she was lounging on the bed with a pair of scissors, slicing away at a new pair of jeans.

"What in Hades are you doing, now?" David asked perplexed.

She smirked. Naturally, he would find the idea of wearing shredded jeans abhorrent. That fact made her project all the more enjoyable, and she began to whack away with renewed glee. "That's none of your business," she reminded him curtly. "But, just for your edification, I'm doing my own thing, for a change."

"And doing your own thing requires the destruction of perfectly good clothes?" he asked dryly. "Hell, Gina, you've done nothing but destroy clothes since I got here. What do you want to be, anyway, a fabric terrorist—or maybe just a nudist?"

"I think nudists call themselves naturalists, these days," she corrected laconically. "But, no, I don't think I'll become a naturalist—unless it will get you to leave!" she added, new hope in her voice.

He laughed. The sound of it seemed almost genuine, and she looked up at him, surprised.

"If you decide to run around here naked, you'd have one hell of a time getting rid of me," he told her honestly. Then, his face once again devoid of amusement, he added, "But you're going to have one hell of a time getting rid of me, anyway."

She clamped her jaws tight. Darn him! Why did he have to have the persistence of a mule? Why hadn't she foreseen this possibility? Why hadn't she known about California's confounded community-property laws? Why did he have to stand there, looking so serious, watching her with those hooded, bedroom eyes?

She cleared the strange knot that had formed in her throat. "Do you mind?" she asked a little hoarsely. "I'd like to try these on—see how they fit."

"Why? Aren't you going to burn them?"

"Of course not." She waved him out the door. "I told you I'm through with hidebound conservatives. Go 'way."

He simply stood there. "It's my bedroom. Remember?" he reminded her, obviously prepared to be an obstacle.

She exhaled distractedly and flounced around turning her backside to him. Quickly she removed her navy walking shorts, exposing her bikini-clad bottom to his gaze as briefly as possible. She slipped on the jeans, pleased with the mutilated effect she'd created.

"Very Dadaist," he offered darkly.

She turned back, her brows knit. She hated it when he used words she didn't understand, but she refused to admit that she had no idea what he'd meant.

"Dadaist—a meaningless, nihilistic art form," he informed her coolly, knowing her all too well.

"Thank you Mister Funk and Wagnall's," she muttered. "But allow me to remind you that I've dropped your course."

She thought she saw him flinch, but he went on, apparently undaunted, "No doubt you're a disciple of the Freddie Krueger school of slasher haute couture."

She was surprised. "How do you know about the Freddie Krueger slasher movies?"

He shrugged. "Even intellectuals hear occasional rumblings from the prosaic, outside world."

"Prosaic," she sniffed scornfully. "That would be your opinion."

"I read somewhere that Freddie Krueger had lost some of his popularity, and that horror enthusiasts are turning to darker, more psychological thrills in the nineties."

"Must you always insist on force-feeding me your stuffy insights? I couldn't care less!" she blazed. "Turn around, David!"

He frowned, puzzled.

"Please!"

"Why?"

With a groan, she relented. "Oh, never mind. Spinning to once again present her back to him, she stripped off her pin-stripe shirt. Deftly she removed her bra, not surprised to hear a low intake of breath from her husband— whom she knew to be highly sexual and aroused quite effortlessly. She gritted her teeth, hoping she hadn't unleashed a horny monster she couldn't handle—especially considering her own month-long celibacy.

Realizing she'd been rash not to retire to the bathroom for her striptease, she hurriedly donned a cotton-knit T-shirt.

When she turned to face him, David seemed a little pale, and there was a muscle jerking in his jaw.

His eyes roamed restively over the stretchy lilac fabric. The feminist message I Am Woman was emblazoned across his wife's liberated breasts. David's gut tightened with painful longing. He was afraid to try his voice to mention that the phrase was wholly redundant in Gina's case.

"There," she sighed, grinning wickedly at his uneasiness.

"Comfortable now?" he managed, his voice tight.

"Don't I look comfortable?" she asked brightly, stretching her arms languidly over her head. "And you?" She was blatantly taunting him and they both knew it. Deep in her heart, Gina felt that David wouldn't do anything she didn't want him to. This was a rotten thing for her to do. But then again, he'd done a rotten thing to her by moving into *her* lighthouse! A little good old sexual frustration would serve him right!

David could see the calculating gleam in her eyes and valiantly resisted the temptation to throttle her then and there. His body had reacted vigorously to the immodest display of those soft curves that he missed and craved so. He'd meant to thwart her by not turning around, but his plan had backfired badly. All he had to do was look at the self-satisfied smile on her face to know that he'd lost this round.

He sagged imperceptibly against the door frame. "Me? Not comfortable?" he responded as steadily as his physical condition would permit. "Why? Don't I look comfortable?"

2

"WHAT ARE YOU DOING now?" David asked, his patience ebbing fast.

Gina emerged from the bedroom closet with an armload of bedding. "I'm getting everything I'll need out of your bedroom so that I don't have to come back in here tonight."

He pursed his lips. Gina could tell he was perturbed. He always pursed his lips in a last-ditch effort to keep from saying something unpleasant. She inched carefully past him as he leaned against the doorjamb. "Go ahead and say it, David. It can't make things any worse between us." She dumped the bedding on the couch. "But if you're going to stand there looking like a flounder, you'll have to shout it, because I plan to fix myself some dinner."

She flung herself away from him into the kitchen, her shredded jeans leaving little of her hips and long, shapely legs to the imagination. David's eyes narrowed. Who was this braless woman in the lacerated clothing? Certainly not Gina Baron, his compliant wife.

He hadn't moved when she began to bang pots and pans around. Somehow the cacophony of noise she was setting off roused him from his befuddled stupor. Here he was, with his wife, but separated from her by a stupid piece of electrician's tape! No one back at AEI would believe this. Damnation! He didn't believe it. With renewed determination, he walked into the kitchen. "I haven't eaten all day," he announced over the noise. "What are you having?"

She looked askance at him. Ignoring his question, she asked, "May I get something out of the refrigerator? It's on your side."

He scowled. "Get whatever you damn well please. The divided house was your idea, not mine.

She crossed the line. "I'm having a bacon-cheeseburger, hash browns smothered in catsup and a double-chocolate shake."

His laughter was sudden and unexpected.

With her arms loaded with the makings, Gina glanced over at him, her face glowering. "What was that for?"

He sobered quickly enough. "You are joking. Aren't you?"

She crossed back over to her side and thudded the ingredients thudded to the counter. "I never joke about bacon-cheeseburgers."

He walked to her, or at least as close as the dividing line would get him. "Honey. The cholesterol. On your last checkup you had a reading of 197. You really need to watch—"

"Don't call me honey, and don't quote cholesterol to me. If you don't like watching me pack my arteries with fat globules, then go back to Boston!" She ripped open the cellophane on the hamburger and began to fashion patties with the zest of a boxer pummeling a defenseless opponent.

After the meat had been beaten into two patties and they were sizzling in their own grease, plus the grease of four strips of bacon, David asked, "Do you have any chicken?"

"No." Back on her side of the kitchen, Gina glopped ice cream and chocolate syrup into a blender and turned it on.

"Any fish?" he shouted over the loud whirring.

"No." She crossed to his side and flipped a patty. "And I don't have any tofu or unprocessed bran, either."

"Do you have anything I can eat?"

She eyed the spatula in her hand and muttered, "Don't tempt me or I might just feed you this!"

A short time later when she'd turned off the blender and poured its contents into a large glass, she heard him clear his throat. He was trying to control his temper. She'd never tested the limits of David's wrath before, and this was proving to be a very interesting experiment. Gina wondered how long he could continue to put up with her antics before he'd explode and kill her. No, she decided, David wasn't the explode-and-kill-a-person type. He was the soul of reason. The reigning king of prudence. He would try to calmly and reasonably dissuade Gina from her wayward path. Exploding—for David—was out of the question. Well, she would just see how far he could be pushed. Maybe, when he reached the point of exploding, he'd realize, at last, that he would never again be in control of Gina Johnson Baron and that he might as well leave.

She heard him pass behind her toward the refrigerator. As she turned the popping bacon, she eyed him covertly. His long, lean body was bent almost double as he scanned the crowded contents. He looked grim and she smiled. There wasn't a green thing in there—nothing fibrous, if you didn't count the chocolate-milk carton—and nothing that would be caught dead within a square mile of a health-food store.

"What's this?" he asked, holding up a plastic tub.

"Penicillin," she quipped. "I grow my own. But, I think it was beef gravy two weeks ago."

He made a disgusted face, putting it back. "I'll pass."

"It's green—well, gray-green, anyway. You're always harping on eating green things."

"Very whimsical," he muttered, renewing his search on a lower shelf. "Don't you have any lettuce or tomato for that hamburger?"

"No. They're vegetables."

"Actually, a tomato is a—"

"Don't say it!" She held up the metal turner in a threatening gesture.

He stood, eyeing her skeptically. "Or what? You'll spatula me to death?"

Disgruntled, she turned back to her burgers and muttered. "It's a thought."

He opened the refrigerator freezer and examined the frosty occupants minutely, finally opting for the lesser of numerous evils. "Do you mind if I have these frozen fish sticks and some chocolate milk?"

She shrugged. "As long as you pay me back."

"I'll go shopping tomorrow. Is the nearest town Maryvale?"

"Yes." She flopped a dripping burger onto a bun and David flinched at the sight. As she dumped the frozen hash browns into the grease, she said, "Don't tell anyone who you are. I prefer to keep our personal problems personal. Maryvale's a small town and I'd like to become involved in civic activities—without the cloud of scandal."

"Scandal? We're married, dammit!"

"Barely," she countered. "And I don't care for the nice people of Maryvale to know about—your visit."

"What do you want me to say? I'm just passing through and I got the munchies for a little snack—two or three raw chickens, several pounds of fish, all manner of vegetables and a chunk of tofu to tide me over until I reach the Oregon state line?"

"Works for me." She turned back to her burger, slapping a slice of cheese on top of the meat and bacon. A hefty dollop of mayonnaise finished it off.

She added her hash browns and doused them with catsup. Obviously appalled, David tensely asked, "Do you have any vegetable cooking spray?"

"No. And the oven's on the blink. Clute, at the hardware store, has the part on order." Gina eyed him with disdain. "For pete's sake, David, just this once try living on the edge. My leftover grease is hot. Use it."

When his fish sticks were done, he joined her at the table, on his side. "How are they?" she asked, knowing by his face that he would rather be eating shoe leather dipped in gasoline.

"Fine," he mumbled.

"I thought you were going to have some chocolate milk."

"Changed my mind. Water goes better with mystery-fried-fish parts." He looked up at her, his eyes somber. "Gina, this is no good."

"Don't blame me," she shot back defensively, understanding instinctively what he meant but avoiding discussing it. "You cooked the stupid fish." His expression was so dispirited that it made her greasy burger hard to swallow. She looked down at her plate, vowing not to allow his expression to taunt her. It wasn't her problem that he didn't want this divorce. It was his. He would just have to deal with it.

"You know I didn't mean the damned fish."

"You'd better mean the damned fish, because there's nothing else for us to talk about." Suddenly losing her taste for bacon-cheese burgers, she dropped the remainder of her second burger to her plate. "Please go away. Your being here looking woebegone at me won't do either of us any good."

"My leaving won't do us any good, either. I left you alone for a month and that did nothing but harm. Look where we are now."

"*We're* nowhere. I'm somewhere, though. I'm starting to live my own life."

"For how long?" he scoffed, eyeing her plate with repugnance. "If left to your own self-destructive devices, you'll have a stroke."

"At least it'll be my decision!" she retorted, jumping to her feet. She grabbed up her plate and glass and left him staring after her as she dumped the leftovers into the trash. "I'm going to bed!" she declared, stamping out of the kitchen.

David, his jaws clamped to keep from saying anything he'd regret, tore his gaze away from her and stared down at his dismal dinner. Gina was going to bed—on the blasted couch! His lips twisted bitterly. And he'd thought the *fish* had left a bad taste in his mouth!

GINA WAS AWAKENED the next morning by the sound of the front door closing. Her eyes flew open, but momentarily she was fuzzy-headed about where she was and why. "Who is it!" she called, sitting up quickly only to cry out and grab at her lower back before slowly and agonizingly lowering herself to the couch.

"Damn!" she heard David's familiar voice growl, and a moment later he was kneeling beside her, his chest bare and glistening with moisture. She blinked away to stare up at the ceiling. Her teeth bared in pain, she demanded, "Where have you been?"

"Jogging along the beach—it's your back, isn't it," he asked, his voice concerned.

A traitorous whimper escaped her lips and she nodded very slowly.

"Want me to rub it?"

She shook her head, continuing to stare at the ceiling. Her back felt like someone had stabbed her with a pitchfork.

"Gina, this is no time to be proud. I know what to do."

"No," she whispered through clenched teeth. "I'm fine." She closed her eyes and began to inch her way up to a sitting position. Her life flashed before her and the idea of dying seemed almost pleasant. When she was sitting upright, she strangled a moan.

"Don't do this," David admonished gently. "Do you have any pain pills?"

"Go away," she ordered, her voice raspy as she pushed up to stand. She wasn't sure she was totally straight, but she hoped David didn't notice.

"Hell, Gina," David persisted, "you look like a poor imitation of a lower primate. For your own sake, let me help you."

She inched toward the bedroom with slow, agonizing steps. "No, thanks, Tarzan. This cheetah just wants to take a shower. Do you mind if I use the bathroom?"

He shook his head at her stubbornness. "Make it a hot bath. Try to relax."

"I'd be relaxed if I'd had my own bed," she reminded him, her voice strained with her effort to show no pain.

He frowned, unable to find any argument. They both knew it was her own willfulness that had driven her to the couch, but rehashing that would do no good now. As her hunched form disappeared into the bedroom, he offered, "What if we divide the bed? Would you share it with me, then?"

The slamming of the bathroom door was his only answer.

Thirty minutes later, Gina emerged from the bathroom, having taken his suggestion, though she would not have admitted it under torture. She amended that—more torture. David was sitting on the edge of the freshly made bed, hunched forward, his elbows on his spread knees. He was still clad in nylon jogging shorts and his running shoes. He looked thinner than he had a month ago, but not so thin that his muscular attractiveness was lessened. When she came out, clad in a short terry robe, he looked up. His lips were pursed, his eyes contemplative.

She had taken her prescribed medication when she'd gone into the bathroom, and after the hot soaking, she was able to stand almost straight. With careful steps, she moved around the bed toward her dresser, retrieving fresh panties.

"I have an idea," David offered.

"I'm sure you do. I, however, am through being interested in any of your flashes of genius."

She was walking slowly and carefully back toward the bathroom when he said, "Remember *It Happened One Night?*"

She didn't face him, but kept her eyes on her objective—the bathroom door. "Oh, please. The doctor said it was a complete fluke that that sexual position you got us into seemed to help my back. So, don't try to talk me into anything—"

"Gina," he cut in, sounding weary, "I was referring to the old Clark Gable movie where he and Claudette Colbert divided their bed with a rope and a blanket. Would you come back to this bed if I divide it like that?"

She stopped her plodding and turned to eye him with distrust. "I don't know a blanket in the world capable of keeping you at bay, David—not when you're— Well, don't try to con me."

He sat up, appearing offended. "I don't attack women, Gina—not even my own wife. You may not realize this, since you've never been a hesitant participant in our sex life, but I've never forced women into having sex with me, and I certainly don't intend to start with you." He unfolded himself to his full height to look down at her. "What do you say?" he asked gravely. "Would you come to bed if I divide it?"

Mutely she met his eyes. After a long minute, she nodded rigidly, deciding she had no choice if she planned to walk erect on a permanent basis.

Averting her gaze, she retreated into the bathroom to dress, missing his faint, half smile.

IT WAS FOUR O'CLOCK in the afternoon when David returned grocery laden, from the small logging community of Maryvale. When he entered the lighthouse, he was met with the most noxious odor that he could ever recall smelling. He went to the kitchen, where the smell was strongest, and was rewarded by the sight of his wife, again braless, wearing a snug T-shirt and the same lacerated jeans. This time the phrase across her back read: A Woman's Place Is In The House—The Big White One In Washington, D.C.

The major difference in her appearance was that her rich brown hair was wadded up in curlers and she was applying some sort of toxic chemical to each dark mass.

"Oh," she said, looking up from her bent position over the sink. "That didn't take very long."

"What are you doing?" David demanded, realizing he hadn't asked that question as many times in the last ten years as he had in the past twenty-four hours.

"Perming my hair."

"But your hair was beautiful the way it was."

She leaned over, letting out a little moan. Her back was rebelling at being bent at this unnatural angle-especially since she'd already mistreated it by sleeping on the sagging couch.

"David?" Gina remarked through clenched teeth, preparing him for yet another of her tests. "Do you recall that time at the physics award dinner, when you were working late so you asked me to join you there?"

He put his two sacks of groceries on the counter beside the stove and began to put the staples away. "Last November? Yes."

"And do you recall how my hair looked that night?"

He frowned. "Yes."

"So do I. It was curly. I'd experimented with a curling iron. But what did you do when you saw me?"

"I was concerned," he defended.

"You looked shocked and you asked me if I'd reported to the police the description of the bum who'd mugged me. My Lord, do you have any idea what that sort of reaction to a new hairdo has on a woman's self-esteem?"

"I was worried, Gina. You looked—well, a little undone. I didn't know that was a—style."

"Well, I had to go through the whole evening enduring your pained look." She made a squinty face, imitating it. "I hate that look. You give a good impression of Mick Jagger when he wails he can't get no satisfaction! It's an anguished, hostile look, and I hate it!"

"Who's Dick Jagger?" David asked, confused. "Is that the Jagger that teaches ancient Mediterranean civilizations at Boston College?"

She squirted more liquid on her head and sighed impatiently. "Never mind. What I'm trying to say is, my hair will always look like I've been mugged now. So, just don't bug me about it."

"Will it always smell like that, too?" he asked morosely, putting groceries away without much interest in where they went.

"I wish it would. Maybe it would drive you away."

He stopped in the act of putting a jar of bran in the refrigerator and turned to look at her petulant profile as he asked, "How can you hate me, Gina, when I love you so much?"

She aimed a bleak glance at him. "I don't—hate you. You've done your best. I'll never forget, just after we were married, when you took me to my first opera. My folks had been plain folks, without much money. And there you were, my Prince Charming, buying my gown, all the accessories, telling the hairdresser how to do my hair. I was in complete awe of you, and of the whole, exciting experience." She paused, frowning sadly. "But, David. I can't go on being a fairy princess forever. That only happens in fairy tales. In the real world, it's boring. Real people want to make their own decisions—even *wives*. To be brutally frank, I can't stand the idea of being your little—'thing' anymore." She had to stop and grab a towel as solution began to drip down her face.

"You're not my thing," he objected.

"That's true—*now*, anyway. I wish you'd get that through your head and go back to your precious students at Albert Einstein Institute and leave me be."

He watched her dab at her face, his mood darkening. Just as he was about to be forced to say something he knew he'd regret, the phone rang, saving him.

"Could you get that, David?" she called, her voice muffled by the towel.

Without any interest whatsoever in the phone, but realizing that a little distance might help, he walked into the
living room and answered curtly, "What?"

"Hello?" A tentative male voice responded. "Is—er—
Gina Baron there?"

"Yes. Who is this?" David demanded, not caring that
Gina would say it was none of his business.

"Uh—"

"I'll take it," Gina said, grabbing the phone from David's hand. Her hair was now concealed beneath a plastic
cap. She lifted the plastic off one ear and took the call.
"Hello? Oh, hi, Paul." She gave David a brief, this-isn't-
your-business look and turned her back on him.

Since the phone was on the end table beside the couch,
David stepped back across the electrician's tape line and
sat down heavily in an overstuffed chair. Who the hell was
Paul, and why was she using such a syrupy voice?

"Oh, really, Paul? The Maryvale Community Theater?
I'd love to be a part of it. Let me know when tryouts begin." She turned around to see if David was listening. He
made no attempt to hide the fact that he was. With a re-
buking frown, she turned away, lowering her voice, "Sure,
Paul. Tonight at seven. Of course, it's still on. Oh, him?
Nobody. Okay. I'll see you then."

David listened with growing anger. He was *nobody?* He
was her husband, dammit! What was she doing? Dating?
This Paul guy was a *date?* Good God! She'd even giggled.
He'd thought he'd educated that little-girl twitter out of her
long ago. Sitting fixedly, he found himself gripping the
arms of the chair as she hung up and hurried back into the
kitchen.

"Who was it?" he asked, as calmly as he could.

"Nobody you need to know about."

He sank back into the marshmallowy cushion and stared straight ahead. If Gina Baron—his wife—thought she was going out with another man, then she was sadly mistaken. He sat there for a long time, trying to appear at ease. He even took up a magazine from a contraption that was a combination ashtray and pipe and magazine rack— apparently left intact from before Grandpa Johnson had died; the magazines were that old. Slipping on his wire-rimmed reading glasses, he pretended to absorb himself in an article, though it was a magazine comprised of fishing and hunting tips—subjects David cared nothing about.

As time dragged by, he found himself learning more than he would ever care to know about tying flies for trout fishing. At around six o'clock, Gina passed by, humming. Her hair was now dry and kinked up like some drug-crazed rock singer's. He supposed he could be grateful that it wasn't green.

"How do you like it?" she asked, twirling before him.

"Your back must be better," he commented. She smiled, but she wasn't smiling at him, she was smiling to spite him. She thought she was really going to thwart him with this Paul character. He pursed his lips.

"No, David, I mean my hair?"

"I'm glad it's still brown," he offered bluntly.

She laughed gaily, fluffing it with her hands. "That's next week's project. What do you think about yellow-green as a hair color?"

"If your objective is to hide among unripe bananas, then I applaud your choice. Otherwise—"

"Never mind," she cut in, admitting, "Not that I'm trying to please or appease you, but I don't plan to color it. I like it coffee brown, just the way it is."

He snorted derisively. "Finally, we agree on something."

She turned her back on him, calling over her shoulder as her hair flung itself playfully about her shoulder blades. "I'm going to need the bathroom to change. I'll just be a while."

David cursed under his breath.

"A while" turned out to be an hour. David, still dressed in the savvy gray linen slacks and white cable crewneck he'd worn to town, was ready when the knock came at the door. He was up like a shot, dropping both the magazine and his glasses onto the chair as he strode toward the door.

Gina heard the knock and dashed from the bedroom looking young, curly and dangerously sexy in a cotton sundress—braless, again, David noted irritably—as she hurried across the line in her attempt to beat him to their mutual objective. Since he'd been tensed and waiting three hours for this moment, she had no chance of beating him—no chance at all.

"Well, well," David exuded in his perfect host's voice. "Who could be visiting us?"

"It's for me, David," Gina explained breathlessly. But David blocked her way.

When he'd swung the door wide, he flashed a believable smile. "Hello, there. You must be Paul. Come in," he offered, gesturing grandly.

Paul was shorter than David, seven or eight years younger, broadly built and handsome in a blunt, sun-bleached way. Wearing a checked sports shirt, poplin slacks and a thoroughly perlexed expression, the stranger stepped inside the door. Extending his hand he said, "I'm Paul Page. Page Real Estate." He could see Gina and smiled at her as she finally managed to step around the tall obstruction of David Baron.

"Hello, Gina. I like your hair," he said with a smile that telegraphed the fact that he liked a lot more than just her new hairstyle.

She cast David a smug "so there" look as she answered, "Thank you, Paul." She took his arm, unceremoniously swerving him toward the door. "We'd better go—"

"Aren't you going to introduce us?" David cut in, his expression so cheerful it was scary.

Paul looked from Gina to David, then back to Gina.

She shrugged helplessly. "Paul, this is David." She flipped a hand toward David. "David. Paul. Let's go—"

"Paul—" David clamped a hand on the other man's shoulder, halting any possible exit. "How about a drink before you leave. I'd like to get to know you better." He smiled ingratiatingly.

Paul smiled back, but with less enthusiasm. "Well, I suppose we do have some time."

Gina shot David a killing glare, which David deftly ignored. "Fine," he was saying to Paul. "Gina, what would you like to drink?"

Thin-lipped, she stated, "Since neither of us drink, anything containing alcohol would be a little difficult to come up with, don't you think?"

David cocked his head theatrically as though this hadn't occurred to him. "Witless me." He chuckled, looking sheepish. "What was I thinking? So, Paul, how about a glass of carrot juice."

"I—" Paul looked uncomfortable. "I don't think so."

"Turnip tonic?"

Gina rolled her eyes. She doubted that there was even such a thing as turnip tonic. David was contemptible.

"No—I—thanks—" Paul was saying, when David interrupted smoothly, "So, how do you know Gina?"

"I—er—her grandfather stipulated in his will that I take care of the property until Gina could take over. I had the keys to the place." He turned to give Gina a love-struck look that rankled David thoroughly, adding, "She'll sure make a nice addition to Maryvale." Turning back to a scowling David, he asked, "Say, are you Gina's brother or something? I don't remember her saying anything about a brother."

David laughed, and Gina didn't like the sound of it. "Paul, we'd better be—"

"No, I'm not her brother," David broke in. "Actually, Paul, I'm Gina's husband."

The younger man paled visibly. Gina's heart went out to him. "David, don't bully Paul."

"Maybe—I'd better just go," Paul offered, backing toward the door.

Gina grabbed his arm. "Certainly not. We have a date, and I've been looking forward to an evening out with you." Her smile was meant to be encouraging. "David and I are in the process of getting a divorce. You needn't worry about him."

"Oh, absolutely, Paul. Don't worry about me. You two go out and have a good time." David smiled, but his eyes sparked a warning. "I'd appreciate it, though, if you'd have her back by ten. That's when we go to bed. I don't mind saying I hate to sleep without my little love kitten. I'm sure you understand."

Gina coughed, glaring at David. Love kitten? He'd never called her any such absurd name in all their ten years of marriage!

Paul swallowed and tugged at his shirt neck, though the top button wasn't buttoned. "I—er" Paul ventured.

"Let's go, Paul. Ignore him." Positive the worst was over, she tossed her tormentor a beatific smile that was fraught with sarcasm. "Don't wait up, David," she baited.

He broke eye contact with her and shifted his gaze to Paul. Eyes slightly narrowed and one eyebrow lifted in inquiry, he seemed to dare Paul to leave with her, but he said only, "Later..." His smile never faltered.

Though Gina had turned away, intent on making a brisk exit, that one word, stated so quietly yet so cold-bloodedly, sounded like a death threat. She swallowed. Where had her stuffy, bespectacled professor gone? The man behind her had sounded like Dirty Harry or some such bloodthirsty, revenge-seeking, larger-than-life celluloid bad boy!

Paul dragged her to a halt. She looked worriedly over at him. His anxiety-ridden gaze was glued to David's face, and though Gina tried to haul him closer to the door, he wouldn't budge.

"Would—David—would you care to join us for dinner?" Paul asked weakly, obviously not interested in giving this grinning demon any reason to believe he might be contemplating something improper with Gina.

"Why, that's nice of you, Paul," David replied, his smile broadening as though he were really surprised and hadn't manipulated poor Paul into his invitation. "I must admit, I haven't seen much of Maryvale. That might be fun."

"There's not much to see," Paul tried, his expression just short of dismal.

"David, honestly!" Gina protested, aghast at his audacity.

Disregarding her, David said, "Don't sell Maryvale short, Paul. I'm sure it will be the Elysium I've heard it to be."

"Uh—well, whatever. I hope you like family-style eat-ing," Paul remarked as David opened the door for both Paul and Gina to precede him.

"We love it," David assured him, slicing Gina a look that told her that he was going to make sure she never got away with this sort of trick while he was physically able to stop her. He added acidly, "After all, we are a family—right, Gina?"

With high hostility, she shot out, "Temporarily."

"Well—uh—it's good food, anyway," Paul managed, sounding as though he wished he was anywhere else—like being devoured in a shark feeding frenzy.

Continuing to glare at David, Gina declared, "Paul, David will be glad to pick up the check, tonight. Won't you, David?"

"I'd be delighted, Paul," David offered, sounding all too satisfied with himself.

"Thanks," Paul mumbled, tugging at his collar again.

Gina was livid. She should have known that nothing short of binding and gagging David would have pre-vented this. She sighed with exasperation. Feeling sorry for Paul, she took his arm as they proceeded toward his sedan. When David's hand closed over her elbow, she jerked her arm free of his grip. At least, she *tried* to jerk free. Angry and feeling defeated, she cast his smug profile a murderous look. It was all too clear that freeing herself from David Baron's domineering possessiveness would be even tougher then freeing herself from his tormenting hold on her arm.

3

TO GET TO MARYVALE, the closemouthed trio had to travel nine miles through the untamed grandeur of three-hundred-foot-tall redwoods and unspoiled greenery. The road snaked back and forth around canyons, narrow ravines and over rickety bridges.

"Maryvale is a town of about seven hundred hardy souls: big-boned, good-natured descendants of Swedes and Finns who came to Northern California to fell the giant hardwoods." Gina was reciting from a real-estate brochure she'd found in Paul's glove compartment. The deadly silence that had begun their journey was simply too horrible to endure, so she'd decided to opt for babbling noise over deathlike quiet.

"The town is nestled picturesquely among sprawling cedars on a remote switchback, so that California's state Highway 1 runs through the town twice, once on either side of Maryvale Gulch."

Gina, trying to make Paul feel more at ease, turned to him, asking, "I've been wondering about that huge stone library right at the hairpin curve that dissects Maryvale. It's so big for a town of seven hundred souls."

"That's a town joke. I'm surprised you haven't heard about it before now," Paul replied, slanting a brief smile her way. The pleasant expression died when he happened to catch sight of David's sober profile. "Uh—anyway, the Maryvale library fund was left to our town by Mary Bronau, a bighearted, pioneer saloon-keeper, for whom the town was named. The joke is that Maryvale's residents might be rough-and-tumble, backwoods folk, but we're the most well-read rough-and-tumble backwoods folk in the whole state."

Gina laughed. "We are, are we? Well, I guess I'd better get a library card. I'd hate to be too ignorant to talk to my neighbors." As soon as the words had come out, her smile faded and she cast a damning gaze toward David, muttering, "But then, that wouldn't be new for me."

David turned to look at her. "What do you mean by that?" he queried darkly.

When she only shrugged and turned away, the car again was filled with oppressive silence.

It appeared that Paul had opted to take Gina to Mom's Pantry. The coziest place in town, Mom's Pantry was located on the far side of the gulch. The other eatery was nearer, but more boisterous. Known simply as Jake's, its ambience included two pool tables, a jukebox that blared Willie Nelson, and a nightly arm-wrestling competition.

When Paul pulled into an empty parking space outside the rustic log dwelling that housed Mom's Pantry, Gina grimly determined that he had probably thought Mom's would be the more romantic of the two local restaurants. Unfortunately, with David's unwelcome intrusion, poor Paul had been sadly mistaken. A rowdy, four-letter-word-riddled arm-wrestling contest would have been more conducive to a man courting a woman than two hours spent in David Baron's formidable presence.

No one had spoken for ten minutes, and even then, conversation had been limited to a comment by Paul concerning the deterioration of Mason's Bridge as it creaked and groaned under the weight of his midsize car.

The evening air had grown crisp, and Gina pulled her shawl more securely about her shoulders as she and her escorts marched solemnly up the wooden steps. Even once they were inside, struck full force by the room's cheery home-cooking smells, Gina's mood remained gloomy. Both men held one of her elbows, making her feel like part of an angry male sandwich. She cast a stealthy glance at David's ruggedly attractive profile. His nostrils flared—a dead giveaway that he was incensed. She knew that flare. She'd seen him that angry once—at a promising student who'd been caught cheating. But neither his gentle touch on her arm nor the decorous half-smile he wore betrayed his ire.

She looked around the room with its raw walls decorated with antique saws and axes and aged framed photographs of logging as it had been fifty years ago. People seated at tables—mainly the women—stopped talking or listening, whichever the case had been, and turned to look at the threesome as they passed. Gina noticed that more than a few of the local women stared openly at David, smiling if they happened to catch his eye. Her lips thinned. If they only knew that under that aggressively attractive exterior beat the heart of a dictator, they would run like frightened rabbits!

She looked over at Paul, who was keeping up a brave facade as he waved to the café's owner, his Aunt Marta. Paul was too nice a guy to have done this to, and Gina chided herself for not canceling when he'd called this afternoon. It was too bad that hindsight was so much clearer than foresight. Paul didn't deserve being caught in the middle of her marriage's death throes. Sighing heavily, she braced herself for the evening to come, knowing it would border on disaster—and that was her optimistic side speaking.

When they'd been seated at a candle-lit table and had ordered, Paul cleared his throat, drawing both Gina's and

David's gazes. The blond man smiled weakly. "Well, so, er, what brings you out here to the West Coast, David?"

"He brought me some papers," Gina put in, not wanting to get into the subject of David's reluctance to accept the fact that their marriage was over.

"Oh?" Paul responded, looking perplexed.

"Actually, I returned them to her," David corrected, smiling but not bothering to involve his upper facial muscles in the expression, leaving his eyes devoid of pleasantness.

"Oh?" Paul repeated, uncomfortable. Trying to fill an awkward gap, he asked, "So—what is it that you do, David?"

"I'm dean of the physics department at Albert Einstein Institute in Boston," David commented, his smile remaining remote and polite.

"Yes," Gina added. "David has a Ph.D. in quantum physics. If you ever need to know the mass of any given comet charging around in the solar system, feel free to call on David."

"Oh," Paul repeated, nodding gamely. "Then, I guess you're a doctor of some sort."

David shrugged, indicating the affirmative. "Having a Ph.D. is far from unusual in Boston."

Gina's strained laugh was unexpected. "Far, *far* from it! There are more Ph.D.'s per square foot in Bean Town than in any other city in the country—probably, in the universe." Her tone morose, Gina added, "Imagine my delight at being the only non-Ph.D. at any twelve gatherings out of a dozen."

"Nobody cares about that, Gina," David admonished quietly. "You always insist on making such a big thing out of it. Besides, I wanted you to go for your advanced degree. You're the one who insisted on looking for a job."

"Because that's what *I* wanted to do, David! I wanted a job. But, oh, no! A job would cut into my college committee work! Once again, my wants and needs butted up against your wants and needs—and mine lost!"

"Uh—" Paul interrupted faintly, but it was enough to remind David and Gina that they weren't alone. "I— Gina," Paul began looking distressed, "I was wondering what you're planning to do, now that you live in the lighthouse?"

It was apparent that Paul was working hard to find a nonvolatile subject. Regretting her part in his discomfort, Gina vowed to ignore David for the remainder of the evening and concentrate on giving Paul as good a time as possible, under the circumstances. "It's so nice of you to ask, Paul," she assured him, breaking into a compassionate smile. "I'm very excited about my plans."

David noticed her smile and it galled him, but he made no comment, morbidly curious to hear what she had to say—though, as far as he was concerned, any plans she had that didn't include him had no bearing on reality.

"Well," Gina began, her eyes suddenly alight with enthusiasm, "I've collected some wonderful stories about lighthouses— You see, my family has been in the business of keeping lighthouses for three generations, until my dad decided to become a retailer. Anyway, I'll be working on a folklore book about lighthouses and their ghosts."

David choked on a gulp of coffee and Gina was hard put to hide a grin. Naturally, to David, trying to get a book published that concerned lighthouses and ghosts would be tantamount to suggesting that physics was a passing Yuppie craze.

"That's fascinating," Paul commented eagerly. "Does the lighthouse at Sweetheart Point have a ghost story?"

You ask Gina out again and it might! David mused behind a pleasant mask.

Gina took a sip of water, then shook her head. "Unfortunately, no, but that doesn't keep it from being an inspiring place to work."

Paul nodded at Gina, resting his chin on his hands. He smiled. "I've always liked the lighthouse—and your grandfather. I was sorry when old Pappy died."

"He liked you, too." She reached across the table and touched Paul's elbow. "Did I ever thank you for keeping the place up after he died?"

Paul smiled at her and David scowled. Apparently they had managed to forget his presence. He cleared his throat, noticing with some satisfaction that both their smiles died a sudden death.

Paul subtly moved his arm away from Gina's touch, plainly not caring to incur the taller man's wrath. "It was nothing—part of my job," he mumbled. "Besides my real-estate business, I also hire out to maintain properties. It would be only natural for Pappy's will to stipulate that I handle it until you could take it over."

Gina nodded, withdrawing her hand. David had successfully ended an amicable moment. In spite of her vow to ignore him, she fired a condemning glare his way.

David lost track of the conversation, concentrating instead on a flaw on the rim of his coffee cup. *Dammit.* What in hell was it going to take to get this woman to look at him the way she used to—to smile at him—really smile—with love in those exquisite moss-green eyes? He wanted his open, receptive Gina back. He'd have to give the problem some hard thought. Sanity and common sense didn't seem to be working.

By the end of the evening, when they were delivered back to the lighthouse, not very surprisingly, Paul made no attempt to make lingering conversation. David's nerves were raw. He'd endured Gina's purposeful neglect all evening with what he'd thought was admirable self-possession, but he didn't plan to allow her to ignore him one moment longer.

The minute they were alone inside the lighthouse, he stated harshly, "That ghost-book idea of yours is the most ludicrous thing I've ever heard of! How do you hope to live? Even if you get it published, it would take years to get royalties. Good lord, woman, you're living in a dream-world!"

Gina spun on him, her face set. "It's my dreamworld, and I want you out of it!" She dropped dejectedly to the sofa. Unable to hide her swelling anguish for one second more, she accused, "At least Paul was interested enough to ask. You've been here for twenty-four hours and you didn't even inquire."

"That's because you aren't staying here," he retorted, his anger no longer in check. "That's because a week from now you'll be back in Boston with me where you belong."

"I won't!" she cried. "I won't go back to that insulated universe where you're always right and I'm a cute little chicken-brain! I tell you, David, it's just not enough for me to spend the rest of my life being The Dean's Wife!"

Exasperated, she ran her hands through her curls, sighing heavily before she could go on. Then, more quietly, more dejectedly, she admitted, "I'm disappearing—being devoured by the force of your will." Sadly, she shook her head. "I want to make a mark of my own, to contribute something."

"Oh, sweetheart," he lamented through a moan. "A lot of women find happiness with the career of simply being a wife."

"Like my mother?" she challenged tearfully.

He looked perplexed. "What is this about your mother, all of a sudden?"

"My mother thought she was perfectly happy being a wife, being dominated by my father. I thought it was perfectly okay, too, when I was growing up. My mother was a funny, witty woman, David. But when my father died, she just shriveled up and died, too. She was forty-two. A wonderful, smart lady gave up and withered away within sixty days of her husband's death. She thought that was just fine. But I lost years of what could have been a wonderful, close companionship with her. Don't you see the catastrophe?"

"She was a quiet, obliging woman," he admitted quietly.

"And is that what you want carved on my headstone?" she asked acidly.

"You're nothing like your mother—"

"I will be. Give me twelve or thirteen more years in your devouring shadow! You'll suck everything that was me into you like a benevolent black hole. You'll do it out of love, but I'll still be gone," she countered. "Let me be me— Gina Johnson Baron, ex-bookstore clerk, bachelor-of-arts grad from Boston College. Give me some credit. If given a chance, I can be more than just an extension of you! I have to explore my boundaries—find my passions. You have physics. Why can't I have something, too?"

"Fine. Find your something. What the hell is so elusive that you can't find it with me in Boston?"

"Freedom from your smothering bondage, David. I tried! For the five years since Mom's death, I tried to get you to help me become more than I was! But you've fought me at every turn. You dictated my college courses. I wanted to major in psychology, but here I am with a completely useless degree in ancient Mediterranean civilizations!

"And since I graduated, you've made excuse after excuse why I shouldn't look for a job 'right now.' And when I went ahead and applied at several places, you advised me why this or that job wasn't right for me—the hours would cut into our entertaining, or I'd be away from home, away from my responsibilities as Pep Club sponsor! I can't live like that any longer. Time's up! I promised myself that by the time I turn thirty, I will be my own woman. Unfortunately, you've proven to me, over and over again, that the only way I can become that woman is to leave you."

He pursed his lips, provoked. "You can't live out here," he growled, hurting. "You don't have any money. Since I refuse to divorce you, don't expect me to finance this crazy enterprise of yours."

"Grandpa left me seven thousand dollars. That'll keep me for a while."

His lips twisted with melancholy. "Not long, Gina. Then what will you do?"

"I don't know, exactly, but I do know I'd rather be locked in a room with nothing but great works of literature and die a slow, boring death having them read aloud to me than go one inch with you!"

He flinched. He'd thought she'd enjoyed their evenings spent with him reading the classics to her. Wounded and filled with painful longing, he muttered, "Darling, over the years, you've seemed contented enough with the 'inches' we've traveled together."

Her face grew hot and she knew she must be crimson. Embarrassed, she retorted testily, "Sex isn't everything, David!" Somehow it had come out oddly breathless, giving away her intense reaction to the mention of their lusty sex life.

The knowing quirk of his lips stirred her more than she cared to admit, so she blurted hastily, "If you're really interested in my plans, maybe I'll just marry Paul!" She knew she was being unfair, but his bringing up their hot-and-heavy sex life had been unfair, too. In truth, she had no more romantic feelings for Paul than she had for—for...

Odd, she'd thought she'd be able to admit that she held no romantic feelings for David, but something deep inside her hadn't allowed her to say it. She toughened herself against any lingering feelings for him, forcing herself to stare at his crestfallen face, but avoiding his troubled gray eyes. "Don't fret about me, David. I'll get along."

"You can't marry Paul if you're still married to me," he persisted, his voice dangerously quiet.

"I won't be married to you. Even a mule, when whipped enough times, finally gets the idea and budges from his stubborn stance! Surely you have the brains of a mule."

She saw torment flash across his face before he looked away; his desolate expression tore at her heart. She was being cruel, and she hated herself for it. "David..." she began, her voice breaking. "I—I don't mean to be harsh. You're a brilliant, good-hearted man. It's just that you aren't good for me anymore." She sighed dispiritedly, adding, "And I don't suppose it's in your nature to change."

She chewed on her lower lip in the deafening silence, expecting him to retort, to defend himself. When he didn't, she added sadly, "You—you've turned me into something that is simply foreign to my nature. Oh," she hurried on, half apologetic, "I know I'm partly to blame because I allowed it, but I was young, inexperienced and anxious to learn." *And madly in love with the correct young professor who walked into my predictable life and swept me into a whirlwind courtship that lasted mere weeks before our blissful marriage*—some malevolent part of her brain insisted on reminding her.

"Once you told me what had first attracted you about me, David. Do you remember what it was?" she asked, in a voice just above a whisper. When he didn't respond, she continued, "You said I was like a bright new penny, before it's been tarnished. I was different from your rigid and formed world—'So refreshing,' you said." She paused, meeting his eyes solemnly before she asked, "Can't you see the irony in that?"

"No," he denied roughly. "I haven't tarnished you, Gina. I've done nothing but give, wanting only what's best . . ." He faltered, frowned, started to go on, but shook his head, remaining silent.

"So, we've come to another impasse." Fighting tears, she whispered brokenly, "If I allowed my—myself to be pulled back into the same situation just because I can't quite rid myself of my affection for you, it would settle nothing." Her words were barely audible now. "I'd—I'd be forced to leave you again, eventually." She hated having to be ruthless, but she had to be unwavering—end this, once and for all. Even though she had a fierce desire to take him in her arms and apologize for her hurtful words, she stood her ground.

Pulling her lips together in a tight line to keep them from quivering, she steeled herself for his verbal attack. Agitated almost to the point of nausea, she waited. It startled her when, instead, he turned away to the narrow fireplace mantel. His wide shoulders had dropped measurably as he began to finger the iridescent inner surface of an abalone shell—one of a striking collection left to her by her grandfather.

David simply stood there examining the half-melon-size mollusk with grave interest, and it began to prey on her nerves that he, for once, had nothing to say. When the heavy silence had grown as painful as the words had been, she announced tiredly, "I'm going to bed."

"I won't allow you to sleep on the couch," he stated in a tight whisper.

Knowing her back couldn't take another night on the sofa, she rejoined, "Will you keep on *your* side of the bed?"

"It's divided."

"That's not what I asked."

With a curse he turned to face her, his narrowed, sparking eyes searing her as he responded coldly, "I know damned well what you asked, Gina. Go to bed. I won't molest you."

She cringed, not only at the rage that burned in his eyes, but at the muscle that had begun to twitch in his cheek. Though his anger was tenaciously controlled, she had never seen David this angry, and the knowledge that he was capable of such fury frightened her. As swiftly as she could, Gina vaulted past him into the bedroom.

DEEP IN THE NIGHT, Gina felt David's hand on her thigh, patting in odd feathery strokes. Even asleep, he recognized her familiar, soft flesh and groaned audibly. Suddenly frightened by her own heated reaction, Gina brushed his hand away, waking him in the process.

When his hand disappeared behind the blanket, she heard his gritted curse, and he sounded charmingly groggy. Because she was sure he'd been asleep when he'd reached for her, she didn't scold him, deciding the less said about the incident, the better.

Yet, even an hour later, Gina could tell from his breathing that David hadn't been able to fall back to sleep. Unfortunately, neither had she. His touch still lingered against her skin like a phantom lover's caress. Finally, irritated beyond words, she got up and took a shower, scrubbing her skin until it was red. She didn't want David's touch to bother her so. What was she going to have to do to get this man to leave?

AFTER A WEEK OF DAVID'S disgruntled presence, Gina was beside herself. Her mental state had swung haphazardly from anger to anguish, exhausting her in both body and mind. He had refused to budge, either physically or in his unyielding attitude. On the eighth day of his punitive visit, at her wit's end, Gina decided she had to do something to get him out of her life forever. What she came up with was extreme, but she was close to losing her mind, having his constant presence draped over her life like a thorn-filled shroud. She had to have him out and gone. Maybe if she'd been less harried, she might have thought better of her plan, but she was frantic.

Hoping to push him beyond his emotional endurance, she chose the only way in which she knew she could be completely successful: sunbathing in the nude. The beach was totally isolated, so she would be displaying herself for only her pompous husband, who had once refused to allow her to swim while on vacation in France because the nearby beach was designated "topless."

It was early afternoon and the weather was perfect for sunning. David had taken up reading in the easy chair. As usual, it was one of his infernal classic tomes. This one, she noticed, was written in Latin. She wondered how much fascination a "dead" language would hold for him, once he realized his wife was sunning in the nude on the beach below. She only wished it was a public beach. David would have a stroke if he even dreamed she would prance around buff-bare among other men. Now, that would really drive him up an ivy-covered wall!

God willing, knowing that he could look but not touch would be the final straw that would send David screaming back to Boston, leaving her to make her own life on this side of the continent.

Dragging a towel coquettishly behind her, Gina slammed the bedroom door, intent on drawing David's gaze. She smiled inwardly to see his eyes widen in what was at first a look of hope and appreciation, but then utter shock as she padded across the living room to disappear out the front door—stark-naked.

It had only taken David enough time to rip off his glasses and launch himself from the chair when Gina reappeared, towel clutched to her breasts as she leaned heavily against the door. Her face was constricted in horror, her body bent over in an embarrassed half-crouch. She sputtered, "David—David, help me...." Motioning behind her, she whispered, "There's a deliveryman coming up the walk. He *saw* me!"

David faced her, looking rankled. "What do you want me to do? Have him arrested for making deliveries to a deranged woman?"

She shook her head wildly. "No, just go out there and get the package. I couldn't face him!"

He frowned at her as she struggled to cover herself with the towel. "What did you think you were doing, Gina?"

Halting her fumbling for a moment, she looked up at him, tilting her chin as haughtily as her humiliation would allow. "I can sunbathe on my own beach if I want to, can't I?"

Before he could respond, there was a knock at the door. Gina ran around behind David and cowered there. "You go," she whimpered. "I'd die before I could face that man."

He exhaled heavily and disappeared outside. After a few seconds he was back with a padded envelope. Tossing it on the couch, he observed dryly, "Well, you made that man's day. I have a feeling you'll be getting a lot of deliveries—whether they belong here or not."

She groaned. "What did he say?"

David shrugged his wide shoulders, plunging his hands into his trouser pockets. With a grave expression, he muttered, "The guy said I was damned lucky."

Gina, her towel wrapped around her now, picked up the package and began to open it—more to avoid David's unhappy gaze than with any real interest in what was inside.

"What is it?" he asked grimly.

"It's a book I ordered." She pulled it out. "It's called *The Dominating Male And How to Rid yourself of Him*."

He made a disgusted noise. "I've heard of that book. It was reviewed with the comment that it rivals the extramarital affair for breaking up marriages."

She dropped the book on the couch and faced him squarely, retorting, "That book can't be blamed for breaking up something that's already broken—as it is in our case." With that, she swept past him, resolute in going forward with her original plan. But before she made another reckless exit, she peered out the door. The thought flitted across her mind that she might not be quite ready for public nude beaches, after all.

She crept onto the porch and craned her neck around to the side of the lighthouse to be sure the truck was gone before she pulled the towel from her body and strutted down the stone walk toward her picket fence and the rock ledge beyond.

"Do you mean to tell me you're actually going to sunbathe naked?" David called after her.

"What does it look like?" she chided. "And don't get any ideas, David. My body is my own and my nudity has nothing to do with you anymore."

He gritted his teeth. He'd spent the week being frustrated in more ways than one over this woman and her calculated plan to drive him crazy. Well, if this was the newest attack in her scheme, then she may have struck upon the perfect way. He didn't know if he could just stand there watching her, seeing her lovely lithe body—her slender arms, her firm, creamy legs, her satiny breasts....

He was half bent over with lust as she vanished below the rim of the cliff. The woman was really going to do it! With a raw curse, he decided that little Mrs. I-Dare-You-to-Touch-Me had taunted him once too often in the past week. Ripping off his tie, he headed out the door. So, she wanted to play games, did she? Well, two could play at this one. He could never recall a time when she'd resisted the invitation of his naked body, and he didn't plan to pass up an opportunity to let her try.

By the time he'd reached the sand below and was sure Gina had turned her aghast attention on him, he dropped one maroon suspender and then the other. The sound of his slack's zipper was loud even against the sound of the lapping waves.

"What do you think you're doing?" Gina cried out.

His smile was so devilish, it sent a shiver of alarm up her spine.

"David—don't you dare!"

With provocative disobedience, he allowed his white slacks to slide down over a shirttail that whispered of hidden, masculine delights. On down, down those plaguing trousers slid, revealing powerful thighs, to fall at last in a shameless heap around sexy, totally unprofessorial calves.

4

GINA CAME UP ON ONE elbow, staring as David stepped out of his trousers. Standing there clad only in a pin-striped dress shirt, Jockey shorts and socks, a devilish glint sparkled in his eyes. Sexy and half naked, he even managed to make removing his socks an erotic experience. Gina blinked and licked her lips nervously—or was her action in some small way anticipatory?

She stiffened as he began to unbutton his shirt. "David. This is ridiculous." Bolting up to a sitting position, she demanded, "Get back into the house."

He tossed her a half grin ripe with wicked defiance. "It's my beach, too," he reminded her as the shirt fluttered to the sand, revealing a sculptured chest to which the sun paid golden homage. Planes of light and shadow mischievously shifted as he moved his body. A simple lift of a shoulder or the slow, contrived turn of a hip proved to be more seductive than any lewd bump and grind might have been.

David's striptease, though smooth and alluring, was relentless in its aim, mounting to a blistering crescendo. She swallowed, not happy with the heat that had begun to gnaw in the pit of her stomach.

Clad only in Jockey shorts, David hooked a thumb under the elastic band at his waist, threatening her with an explicit wink as he began to tug the fabric down.

She stared with the same fascination as one might watch a cobra as it prepares to strike. The well-developed muscle that angled across his hipbones became exposed, and then the taut, rounded rise of the hip itself. The dark swirl of hair that had tapered off below his chest, began to broaden again. To save herself, Gina forced her gaze away and, dragging her watery limbs beneath her, she struggled to her feet, sputtering, "I—I think I'll go for a swim."

"Getting hot?" he queried as she scurried and stumbled toward the lapping water.

She frowned, pretending to ignore the taunt in his words, concentrating on ignoring him. Unfortunately, some unmanageable part of her consciousness insisted upon noting the exact instant those Jockey shorts hit the sand. She had no idea that her peripheral vision was so encompassing. She wished, at that moment, that she were more inclined toward tunnel vision—at least where one wanton doctor of physics was concerned.

The cold seawater hit her calves and she gasped. But since her naked husband was approaching on her left, she decided a cold dip was preferable to a hot tumble, since the hot tumble would cure nothing—except a disquieting flame searing a familiar region deep within her.

As she surged into the water, she instinctively spun away from the wind-tossed spray. It was a bad move, for when she turned her back on the spray, she was put in full view of David, who had reached thigh depth in the water. Immediately her gaze was drawn to an area below his waist where the sun glinted unexpectedly, and she sucked in a harsh breath that had nothing to do with the chill of the surf against her bare backside.

He stood there under the bright midafternoon sun—his shoulders broad, sunlit, with more than just his stance gorgeously erect. His burnished hair was tossed across his brow by the wind; his thighs were damp, bold and strong. Seeing him there like that, dynamically aroused, he seemed more than merely human. He was something out of mythology—perhaps Poseidon, the Greek god who ruled the sea. And as he looked now, she could well imagine that, with such a scepter, he could rule very, very satisfactorily!

Hating the unruly thought, she decided to put considerable distance between them. In a rush to get away, she stumbled, falling backward into the frigid depths. Floundering, struggling for breath, she sucked in salt water instead of precious air. By the time she realized she'd been lifted clear of the suffocating brine and could stop flailing, she was too spent from coughing to fight the fact that David was holding her in his arms, his expression a dark mixture of ill temper and worry.

"Dav—" she broke into another sputter of coughing "—put—me—"

"Not this time, darling," he vowed, hauling her toward the beach.

Gina cleared a heavy tangle of dripping-wet curls from her face and squinted up at him. His set features were spangled with water from her thrashing. "I'm—I'm not through swimming yet," she finally managed, only to see his face soften minimally.

"Is that what you were doing?"

She coughed again. "I just fell—anybody can fall. Now I'm going to swim."

"We can swim later."

"Later?" She stiffened with distrust. "Why not now?"

"Because, my dear," he whispered as he knelt on the sand and lowered her to her towel. "Right now, we're going to make love."

As her hips came to rest on the terry cloth, she pressed her hands to his chest. "We're not!" Somehow the remark didn't come out so much as a command as an expression of awed surprise.

He smiled down at her, and she was fascinated by the water that spangled on his lashes, both upper and lower. He had the most beautiful eyes of any man she'd ever seen.

"I've missed you, Gina," he whispered before lowering a tentative kiss to graze her upper lip.

The sweet restraint of his lips sent a shiver of uninvited delight along her spine, completely defusing her planned resistance. His face above hers again, he watched her for a moment, his expression open, loving. She was suddenly lost in his spell, and with an almost-eager expectancy, she found herself tracing with her tongue the place where his mouth had been. Relishing the salty warmth of it, Gina searched his face, her eyes aglow with reluctant invitation.

For David, her quiet observation was invitation enough.

When he once again lowered his lips to hers, her body was all too eager for his touch, her mind clouded by temporary insanity. David's second kiss was coupled with a gentle settling of his nakedness over hers. A breathy sigh escaped her lips when his body bestowed its message of carnal delights to come.

His name became a pained whimper as his kisses, like honey drops of fire, did their work, heating her to a state of gasping desire.

His hands teased, tortured, drawing from her a hunger to be led astray—beyond her will, her good sense, her life's plan—to be, once again, one with David Baron, her mate and her nemesis.

Not until she was crying out his name, clawing at his back, did David relent in his lusty pillaging of her defenses. He had been an amorous aggressor, without shame or remorse, for he was fighting for his very life—the only

life he desired to live: with Gina. He knew how to move
her, to touch her, to kiss and stroke her. He knew the se-
crets of her nape, her inner wrists, the sensitive hollow of
her back. He knew the sound of her breathing and how to
judge from it the extent of her need for him. He used this
knowledge well. It pleased him when her body responded
wildly to his ministrations, when her legs heeded a natural, earthly call and parted with invitation.

He felt blessed when her nails raked lovingly, desperately, along his back. How long he'd dreamed of such
sweet pain, of such unstrung longing in her trembling
limbs, and of her fragile, thready cries.

Finally, when she was at the pinnacle of urgency, he allowed himself the delight of slipping into the dear moist-
ness of his only love. His moan was one mixed equally
with divine deliverance and repressed pain. Tears came to
his eyes with his reverent relief as she enclosed him within
the carnal embrace of her legs, and they began the familiar, yet ever-new and renewing, lover's dance.

Gradually at first, they relished the exultation of becoming one pulsating being, mending and rejuvenating
themselves within each other. Moved by David's sexual
urgings, Gina experienced the rapture of heightened feelings. She found herself being lifted toward a dizzying place
that she'd prayed never again to know—at least not at
David's expert hands. She was panting, whimpering, but
not with regret—though her mind should have been set in
that direction.

Gina was exploding with pleasure—flesh-rending, ex-
travagant delights that no woman should be able to live
through. Every time David brought her to this white-hot
brink of ecstasy, she found herself believing that only
sweet death could release her from the fuse that his sexual
prowess had ignited. With a cry that frightened seabirds

from their sun-drenched beach, her body shuddered and came apart. David, her David—distressing, disobedient David—had once again catapulted her into the orgasmic firmament.

As she began the long, sweet slide back to sanity, she found herself wondering about the big bang theory. Could it possibly have more to do with how a certain devastating seductive physicist could make love, than any piddling hypothesis about the origin of the universe?

"What's funny?" he asked, sounding charmingly hoarse and breathless.

She hadn't realized she'd smiled, let alone released a low giggle. Opening her eyes, she encircled his shoulders more tightly with her arms and sighed. "Oh—obviously I've been married to a physicist too long. I was just thinking of the big bang."

He looked confused at first, and then his expression softened into a crooked grin. "I'll take that as a compliment."

Unable to help herself, she lifted her head and kissed his chin. "You're a very bad boy, you know," she admonished softly. "This wasn't on my list of things to do today."

He settled his powerful thighs more comfortable—still secure, deep inside the warmth of her body—and retorted with a knowing grin, "Yes, it was, Gina. Did you really think prancing around naked would drive me away?"

She squinted up at him, trying to understand herself, her own motivation. "I really—I . . ." She bit her lower lip. "I don't know." The last remark was barely audible.

"Yes, you do, Gina," he insisted, shifting slightly and drawing from her a gasp of pleasure. "Just as I know what we're going to do now."

She swallowed, her body reacting with such heat and renewed desire to his sly movement that she was appalled with herself for allowing him to manipulate her so easily. But before she could remind him that they were in the process of getting a divorce, and that her nudity had been nothing more than a bad miscalculation today, and that things were no different, she was sighing again, reveling in his passionate, wicked pursuit of their mutual ecstasy. She mumbled no words of wretched regret, harbored no thoughts of bitter remorse; she only cried the soft cries of a woman delighting in a fulfilling sexual adventure.

Some time later, they lay there, spent, their bodies blushed with passion against the pale sand. David teased the lobe of Gina's ear and she stirred from her contented half-slumber. With his teeth nipping her earlobe and his hand resting on her stomach, he murmured, "You know, darling, these next three weeks will make a wonderful second honeymoon before we have to get back for the fall semester."

Gina, now full awake, turned to study his handsome face, softened with satisfaction at having her lying there so docile and deliciously naked beside him.

"But..." she began, but her voice faded. How could she break his heart? My God, her body still glowed with his lovemaking. How could she tell him there would be no second honeymoon?

He grinned at her as he came up on one elbow. Languidly he began to trace along her rib cage, drawing a shiver of new delight from her. "I know what you're going to say, love," he drawled softly. "While we're here in California, we should run down to Los Angeles. You'll need new clothes. After all, you can't go back to AEI looking like a hippie—"

She put her hands over his, stopping his sensual trek along the undersides of her breasts. "Wait a minute," she began again, this time more sternly. There was no putting this off. She drew away, coming up to a sitting position. "David, please. Nothing has changed between us."

She watched the happiness—the trace of smugness—fade from his face, to be replaced by confusion. "Gina," he said quietly, "that's not funny, darling." He moved toward her, and she had to jump to her feet to avoid being taken into his arms. When she did that, his expression grew desolate. "You're not joking," he mumbled, disbelief ripe in his words.

She shook her head, her damp curls slapping her shoulders, as though even her hair were angry with her decision. But she didn't back down. Instead, she backed away, retorting as evenly as she could, "David don't you understand? One little tumble on a beach won't set things right between us. You know that sex has never been our problem."

He was standing now, too, his towering nakedness a beautiful, terrible thing to witness. She made herself focus on the ocean's restive tide.

"But Gina—we have so much, together. You can't propose to throw it all away just because you're feeling a little discontented. Everyone goes through phases. This fear about being like your mother—it will pass as you mature."

She flung herself around to face him again. "Don't you dare say I'm not mature! I'm nearly thirty. Don't treat me like a child. I'm not your child!"

"I know that," he growled, his disappointment nudging him toward outright anger. "Hell! What we just shared should damned well prove that I see you as much more than a child!"

"Sex, again! Do you realize that sex is the only human endeavor where you consider me your equal?"

He ran a hand through his hair and exhaled heavily. "That's asinine."

She stared at him unhappily. "No, it's not. Remember when we were redecorating the house and you rejected every single one of my ideas?"

He shook his head, exasperated. "Gina, the house is Victorian. You wanted to do our bedroom in a preposterous black-and-gold New Age theme. You would have hated it in six months."

"It wasn't New Age. It was a blending of Art Deco and high tech. Mr. Inez said my ideas were a sensuous union of engineering and styling."

"Mr. Inez drapes himself in pink chiffon and wears an amethyst in his nose."

"That doesn't make him a fool."

"It doesn't make him a competent decorator, either."

She muttered an oath and spun away. "There's really nothing for us to talk about. Just leave me alone."

He stood there, stiff with incredulity as he watched her nude posterior wagging away. He loved her—loved her delighted laughter, her teasing lips, her unique sense of humor. He recalled sadly what she'd said the other night. It was true. He had fallen in love with her partly because of her openness, her receptiveness, her willingness to try new things. But, blast it! Did one of the new things she was willing to try have to be *divorce!* He wouldn't allow her to divorce him, the little hippie witch. He'd make her walking out as hard as hell!

GINA HAD REFUSED to speak to him for a full day. It had been so damnably quiet in the lighthouse that he even welcomed the music that she had blaring from her cassette player. The sound issuing from the tape was raucous, and the group's lyrics were off-color, but at least it was something. He hated her silence and her dogged capacity to ignore him. It was a talent he hadn't realized she'd possessed—this stubborn, iron will of hers. He found himself grudgingly admiring her for it. She was strong. Maybe stronger than he'd given her credit for. But that new knowledge wasn't giving him any comfort right now.

He looked up from his copy of *Physicists' Weekly*, and peered at her, her legs tucked under her on the couch as she thumbed through a thick file folder she'd unearthed from an old bureau that had been stored beneath the dilapidated circular staircase that led up to the lighthouse tower.

He cleared his throat, hoping she'd look up. She didn't. She merely kept thumbing. Every so often, she'd pull out a sheet of paper and add it to a growing stack of pages.

He gave up and asked, "What are you doing?"

She kept thumbing as though he weren't there.

The singer screeched on. Apparently somebody wanted sex very badly from somebody else. David grimaced, knowing exactly how the lust-stricken singer felt.

"I said," he tried a little louder, "what are you doing?"

She didn't look up, but she stated sharply, "I'm working on my book."

He scrutinized his beautiful malcontent, clad in a scanty T-shirt and a pair of faded shorts, and he scowled. "Your ghost book?"

She peered over at him. "My lighthouse-folklore book."

His lips twisted sardonically. "'The best laid schemes o' mice an' men/Gang aft a-gley.'"

She frowned, stared at him for a minute, contemplating his words. "Gang aft a-gley" was the Scots dialect for "often go astray." She should know, he'd read Robert

Burns's poems to her enough times for her to know them forward and backward. After a long moment while she allowed her ire to fester, she swung around and flipped off the tape player. When she was facing him again, she demanded, "What do you mean by that? That I won't get this book published, that I won't be able to make it on my own?"

He shrugged his broad shoulders, eyeing her somberly. "It's a tough business, Gina. About as tough as making nuclear fusion a feasible energy source by next year."

With a defensive thinning of her lips, she shot back, "I already have an interested publisher."

"That and eighty cents will buy you a cup of coffee."

With her face set, she declared, "'Oh, wad some power the giftie gie us/To see oursels as others see us!'" With that, she jumped up and headed toward the door. When she'd opened it, she turned back just long enough to fling two words at him. "You bore!" she shouted, and dashed outside.

The slamming of the door echoed in his brain for a very long time, but not as long as the crushing insult. Bore? He closed his eyes. Absolutely. He *had* been a condescending bore. He sat back heavily, allowing his scientific periodical to slide to the floor. What in hell had he thought he was doing when he'd provoked her? What did he think she was? Some kind of masochist who loved to be hurt and who'd come rushing into his arms for insulting her like that?

He had no excuse—only that he'd been desperately unhappy, and had tried to hide his misery behind sardonic wit. The truth was, all he wanted in the world was to know how to love her the way she wanted to be loved. But right now, all she seemed to want from him was for him to leave her alone.

He didn't know how to ask for her love. His father had been a tough-minded man who'd never shown much softness to either David or his mother. Might Meant Right! had been Robert Baron's iron-fisted credo, and it had done his son more harm than good.

Not wanting to be like his father, but knowing he was more like him than he cared to admit, David had always tried to use kindness in his relationships, depending on reason and instruction to show how much he cared. For ten years, he'd thought his efforts had broadened Gina's horizons and drawn her close to him. Clearly, he'd been wrong, and he was at a loss as to what to do now.

One thing he had learned at his father's knee was that a Baron couldn't beg, couldn't belittle himself. *Dammit!* He'd find a way to win her back—without groveling.

Feeling empty, he got up and crossed the room to look out the window. Far below him, on the beach, he could see her rigid form as she tramped away, wind whipping her hair. Staring at her he saw something he hadn't noticed in a long time. Though stiff with anger, her shoulders were beautifully erect—as they had been when he'd first met her. Strange. He hadn't realized, until now, she'd lost a fraction of that splendid, proud stature over the years. He'd loved that confident stance of hers and felt a surge of delight to see it had returned. With a gruff, ironic grunt, he tried to shake off the feeling. He didn't want to be glad about anything she'd begun to do since she'd moved away from Boston!

Heading briskly along the beach now, she looked as though she was being chased by the devil. His lips quirked with melancholy. Perhaps she was—and he was the demon at her heels. That was the last thing he wanted to be to his proud, strong Gina. Why had his life turned into such an ironic mess?

As he watched her, he was surprised to see that she'd begun to drag an old rowboat toward the water. Even from where he stood, the boat didn't look seaworthy. Without stopping to think about it, he bolted from the lighthouse and headed off after her.

By the time he'd descended the stone steps and was loping along the sand, she was clambering into the boat. David shouted, "What do you think you're doing?"

She settled into the weathered craft and took up the oars before tossing him a defiant glance. "Leave me alone, David!" she called. "I can row out to Sweetheart Island if I want. Don't bother me. *I want to be alone!*"

He was breathing heavily by the time he reached the place where she'd entered the water. Fully dressed, he didn't relish plunging into the surf after her, but he had a bad feeling about the boat. "I don't know, Gina. I'm not sure what you're doing is a good idea."

"Shut up, David. Stay out of my life!"

She was rowing erratically, but managing to move away from shore. By now she succeeded in escaping to almost twenty yards out.

Knowing her present state of mind, if he persisted in arguing, she might decide to spend the night on that tiny island to spite him. The nighttime chill would do her no good, since she was wearing such a skimpy outfit. He clamped his jaws shut, and against his better judgment, watched her row farther and farther away.

Gina was near tears. She'd managed to hold them back all day, managed to keep from letting him see how terribly torn she was feeling. Yesterday's romp in the sand had done calamitous injury to her determination to change her life.

He was so gentle, so sensitive to her needs when they were naked in each others arms. She was sure that there were many marriages that would be made perfect if other men knew how to please a woman the way David could please. If only her husband could be as sensitive to her needs out of bed! She struggled to control the wobbling boat, rowing unevenly through the ocean's swells. She was no sailor, and her efforts were marginally successful at best.

Tears blurred her vision, and the tiny sand island grew indistinct in the distance. She needed to get away and be alone so that she could cry—sob, scream, tear at her clothes—until David was out of her system. She couldn't allow yesterday to color her thinking. If she did, he would lure her back into his silky web with soft words and expert loving, and there she'd be, trapped again, to serve out her life—lost, invisible.

She'd fallen in love with him for his bold aggressiveness, but it had become all to clear to her that for a man to be successfully bold and aggressive, his mate had to be constantly weak and submissive. She forced her mother's face into her mind's eye, holding it there, reminding herself what her fate would be if she allowed David to lure her back.

Her mother's eyes had been so dull and hopeless, as she smiled, saying, "My John was everything to me, just as David is to you, Gina. We're so much alike." Chills still ran down her spine when she thought about it. Dead—long before her time because she forfeited her identity to please her man. What a stupid, tragic loss. No human being should abandon themselves to another person: not in body, mind or soul!

Gripping tightly on the oars, she bit off a sob. She couldn't let the same thing happen to her. She wanted to make a contribution to the world—even a small one, but one of her own. She just *had* to do something—create

something, and David must understand that. Now it was
her turn to be bold and aggressive. And maybe it was
David's turn to stand back and listen—however bitter that
lesson might prove to be.

She leaned into her rowing, hauling back on the oars
with all her strength, sniffling and blinking away tears.
He'd stopped shouting after her. That was good. Casting
a quick glance over her shoulder, she could see him there.
Legs braced wide, his hands fisted on his hips, he stood
still, mute, watching her, his expression harsh and unhappy.

She turned abruptly away, bent on showing him once
and for all that she meant what she'd said. They were finished. But first, she had to have a good, private cry. She
stopped rowing long enough to wipe her eyes. Shifting for
a better position, she moved her feet wider apart, surprised that when she did, water sloshed over the tops of
her canvas shoes, chilling her ankles.

She looked down, baffled. There shouldn't be water inside the boat! To her horror, she saw that not only was
water in the boat, but it was rising fast. It had come in
suddenly, and hadn't even had the time to soak through
her shoes. Now, seconds later, it had already risen to lap
around her bare ankles.

Rowing was becoming futile as the boat moved slug-
gishly, though she'd never gotten the process all that
smooth before she'd sprung a leak.

The island was about fifty yards ahead of her. She spun
around to stare back at the shore. She jerked off a shoe and
began to bale water from the sinking boat. It quickly became evident that her efforts were too little and too late.
For every shoeful of seawater she tossed overboard, several inches crept up her legs.

She gritted her teeth. She didn't want to call David for help after having told him in no uncertain terms to leave her alone, but she was frightened. Seconds later, the boat slipped beneath the surface. It had listed slightly to the left, and then to the right before it went under with little more than a soft "glug." As her own personal *Titanic* went down, Gina gave out a cry, belly flopped into the water and began her panic-stricken battle toward the beach. Thirty grueling seconds passed as she flailed along. Her eyes stinging with salt, her throat raw from swallowing water, she abruptly stubbed her toe on the sandy bottom.

It came as a shock to her that she was struggling valiantly to survive in what turned out to be three feet of water. When full realization hit, she stumbled to a standing position and began lurching toward the beach. The ocean current nudged her in that direction as though it were taunting her for her foolish hysteria.

Once she reached the beach, bedraggled and very shaken, one shoe on and the other lost, she tossed David a look that was dagger sharp, daring him to say it—daring him to suggest she would have been better off walking out to the island. Okay! Maybe she would have been, but how was she to know the water was so shallow? She'd never chanced going even ten feet offshore before. She believed in the buddy system—that it was dangerous to venture too far out alone—and before David had arrived, she'd been by herself. She couldn't be blamed for her ignorance, and she wouldn't allow any smirking, almost-exhusband to ridicule her for it.

He was standing there, fully clothed. Dry. Pressed. His expression was not even vaguely amused, which was the only thing that saved his life. And, though he was frowning, he did show signs of relief around his mouth, as though he'd spent a little time during her agonizing experience worrying about her.

Pulling her shoulders erect, she glared at him and protested hoarsely, "You could have done *something!* I almost drowned!"

Pursing his lips, he shrugged his hands into his pockets. When he merely continued to consider her with those disconcerting eyes and made no effort to defend himself, she marched by him, refusing to give him the satisfaction of knowing that when she thought she was about to be devoured by sharks, the last thing she'd thought of was David Baron. *Damn him!*

As she stalked away, her one soggy shoe making embarrassing sucking noises, she thought she heard him mutter something. What was it that he'd mumbled, she wondered? Absently squeezing water from her soggy hair, she sloshed off down the beach, trying to decide. It had sounded something like, "Damned if I do and damned if I don't."

5

THUNDER CRACKED, startling Gina from her reverie. She looked up, realizing for the first time that clouds had rolled in. *Odd*, she thought. The temperature must have dropped ten degrees, and, even soaking wet, she hadn't noticed the sudden chill in the air.

As thunder rumbled again, fat drops of rain began to crash and explode about her. She started to run along the beach to the lighthouse. Just why, she wasn't sure, since she was already soaked to the skin. The rain wasn't likely to ruin her tangled coif or her drenched clothing. Maybe it was just the years of conditioning to dash inside when it started to rain that prompted her flight. Or maybe it was because she could hear David's thudding footfalls approaching rapidly from the rear.

It had probably taken him a few moments of thinking about it—allowing his fury and frustration to rise—before he'd finally decided to give her a good tongue-lashing, outlining to her the error of her ways. Well, she wasn't going to give him the satisfaction; she was going to beat him to the house and then lock herself in her bedroom—his bedroom. Whatever.

In her attempt to keep ahead of David, Gina lost her other shoe. By the time she'd hit the crest of the cliff and was dashing for the picket fence, her breathing was coming in harsh gasps and the rain was pelting down heavily. David, not breathing noticeably hard, was pulling slightly ahead. She groused inwardly over the fact that she'd quit jogging when she'd left him. Plainly, she'd gotten badly out of shape in the last five weeks.

When he made the gate, David surprised Gina by leaping it with the grace of an Olympic hurdler. It rankled her to have to stop and fumble for the latch. By the time she'd made the door, he was already there. But he hadn't gone inside. Instead he was standing on the covered porch staring down at something.

Gina halted, panting, just behind him. "What are you—looking at?" she wheezed.

"I think it's a cat," David observed, breathing a bit heavily himself. "But it's damn ugly, if it is."

The ball of bedraggled gray-and-white fur was cowering and hissing in a dry corner, half hidden behind a potted geranium.

Gina knelt, forgetting that she was now chilled and soaked through. "Oh, the poor thing," she cooed, trying to sound as unthreatening as possible. "David," she whispered, "do you have any tuna fish in your larder of disgusting health food?"

"I have some water-packed white-chunk."

She peered up at him. "I don't care if it was packed by marauding hordes of wild-eyed members of Greenpeace. Would you open a can? This poor thing looks half starved."

"It also looks like it would as soon kill you as look at you," he observed darkly.

She glanced up at him, noticing for the first time that he was now soaking wet, too, his Yuppie attire plastered to his body. She couldn't help but smile wryly. "You don't look so good yourself."

His frown deepened. "How bad do I have to look for you to care about me?"

With an unhappy sigh, she turned back to inspect the cat. "Please—just get the tuna. Seems like this poor animal was dumped. He needs our help."

He decided not to argue. Turning to go, he muttered, "I'll get the fish but I don't think it's a good idea. That thing could have rabies or something."

Fifteen minutes later, the stray was inside the kitchen, stomach full of water-packed tuna. Contentedly cleaning his fur, he was purring, curled up on David's lap. David, having changed into dry clothes, was far from contented, however. He sipped a cup of decaf and scowled down at the unkempt beast that had forsaken Gina's cooing ministrations and leaped determinedly into his lap a short time before. "Why the hell my lap?" he growled.

Gina, who now wore jeans and a dry T-shirt, her hair wrapped in a towel, was fixing herself a hot dog. "He likes you, David. Why he chose you over me, though, I can't imagine."

"I hate cats."

She spread mustard over her bun and grinned at him in spite of herself. "No, you don't, David. You just haven't ever been around animals. All men think they hate cats until they're around them."

"I've been around animals. I was born on a ranch."

"Yes, but you were a little boy when you went to that boys' school in England."

His expression, as he met her gaze, was skeptical. "Nevertheless, this is the ugliest cat conceivable. Not to mention the fact that it has only half a tail."

Gina's smile faded and she looked suddenly sad. "All the more reason why the poor little guy needs love. He's had rough treatment at somebody's hands. Look there." She indicated the purring feline. "Why, some food and human warmth is all in the world he wants. It's little enough for one of nature's creatures to ask."

David's expression changed from skeptical to somber, and the gaze he turned on her spoke volumes. He was saying, *All I want from you is a little human warmth, my love.* The plea was so clear, etched in the pain in his eyes, he might just as well have screamed it at her. Unable to deal with his feelings of rejection, she pivoted away and piled relish on her wiener.

When she'd finished constructing her meal and was walking to her side of the divided table, she noticed David absently lay his hand on the cat's back. He was watching the animal, and when it switched from licking its fur to licking David's hand, he murmured, "Dumped, huh? I know the feeling."

Gina heard that exchange, even though it had been low and barely audible. She only wished she hadn't.

Halfway through Gina's hot dog, the phone rang. David looked toward the phone and then at her. The cat didn't stir.

Gina mouthed the words, "I'll get it. You sit."

When she picked up the phone she whispered, "Hello? Oh, hello, Paul. Whispering?" She laughed, raising her voice to a normal level. "Sorry. We found a cat. It's sleeping, but I guess whispering is a little much."

David was now listening intently. Paul? What in the hell did he think he was doing, calling back? David had thought the last time they'd seen him would be the very last. Paul had been miserable, poor guy. Looking back on it, David felt a little badly—not badly enough to invite the young milksop to dinner and apologize, but a little badly.

"Oh, sure, Paul. That's nice of you. We'll be here." Gina started to hang up, but had a thought. "Oh, Paul? Could you pick up some cat food and a litter box? I'll pay you when you get here. Thanks." She hung up.

David couldn't stand it. Sleeping cat or no sleeping cat, he called out, "He's coming out here?"

The cat's eyes opened, but only languidly. He stretched, yawned and went back to sleep.

Gina returned to the kitchen. "He's bringing out the part for the oven that's been on back order. Clute Bradly's wife has gone into labor, so he's closed down the hardware store for the day. Paul said Clute gave him instructions about how to install it and asked him to deliver it since Paul was coming out this way to look over some property. Naturally, being an agreeable man, he said he'd do it."

Thunder cracked again muffling David's response. Gina had a feeling it was just as well. She cautioned, "You're going to be civil, aren't you? Paul didn't sound too thrilled to do this, so be pleasant."

David decided he'd had enough cat-sitting for a while. Just knowing that Paul was dropping by set his teeth on edge, and he felt the need to move, to pace, throw something. Deciding the cat would be better off out of his reach, he carried it into the living area and put it on his easy chair. So completely blissful, the stray had become nothing but a trusting lump of fur. When he was deposited on the chair, he conformed to the cushions as though the chair had been made for its thin carcass, and went instantly back to sleep—purring.

"How long is he going to be here?" David asked as evenly as he could manage, though jealousy was hammering like a fist in his belly.

"He offered to fix the oven," Gina explained, following him into the living room. "He's a sweet man. Don't growl at him."

David faced her, his eyes narrowed and glittering. "I won't growl. I never growl," he growled.

She shook her head, frowning. "I won't have you browbeating my friends."

"I don't browbeat, either," he protested. "I'll be the perfect host." He paced to the door that led to the lighthouse tower and then back before he added, "Gina, couldn't you at least go put on a bra?"

She bristled. "Don't tell me what to do."

He closed his eyes, his jaw working in agitation. After a minute he mumbled, "It's a request, damn it. You—you have—nice breasts. I'm not the only man who thinks so, either. I'm sure parcels will soon be piling up on the doorstep, if I read that deliveryman's face right. And unless you're ready to have sex with Paul, don't go braless in front of him.

She opened her mouth to protest, but something stopped her. She told herself it wasn't the fact that he'd just complimented her. She didn't want to be responsive to his gallantries, anymore. No, she insisted her refusal to lash out at him came from a remote, logical part of her brain that agreed with him. She did look a little...wanton, maybe. She'd actually give herself pause a time or two when she'd passed a mirror and had seen her bouncy reflection. If it had been anyone but David sharing the lighthouse with her, she would never have dared to go around so unconfined. Though she didn't like it, she decided to relent on this one point.

With a defiant toss of her head, she marched toward the bedroom. "Well, maybe I'm not quite ready to have sex with him," she offered tersely before she disappeared to alter her appearance for company.

When she'd gone, David breathed a low sigh of relief—not so much because she'd done what he'd asked, but because she'd admitted that she wasn't quite ready to jump into bed with Paul. It was a small triumph, but it would have to do.

Walking over to the inert cat, he knelt down. Stroking its emaciated body, he mumbled, "So—Lump, what fickle female ripped off *your* tail?"

IT WAS ALMOST AN HOUR later when there was a halting rap on the lighthouse door. Gina was leafing through her folder of treasured old lighthouse stories. It had been raining continuously, which had probably slowed Paul's progress. As she put her folder aside, David looked up from his easy chair. Lumper, as they'd decided to call the stray, was once again snuggled in his lap.

Wordlessly, it was decided that Gina would get the door. David, apparently, was going to try to behave.

As the door swung open, Gina's pleasant greeting froze on her lips as she beheld Paul, soaked, mud-spattered and pale. "Good gracious, Paul!" she cried, distressed. "What happened to you?"

He sagged against the doorjamb, his arms clutching a soggy grocery bag.

"Mason's Bridge—it fell in—I was on it when it went down."

By this time, David had joined Gina at the door and was taking Paul's bag from his rigid arms. He set the wet sack down and with a gentle tug on the man's shoulder urged him inside. "What happened to your car?" he asked, once the door was closed.

Paul stared at nothing in particular. "In the gorge. I just had time to scramble out of it and make a flying dash to the side before the whole thing crumbled into nothing."

Gina was stunned. "And you took time to save the cat litter?"

He looked at her, uncomprehending.

She indicated the grocery bag. A sack of cat litter was protruding from its rim.

His lips twitched in a sorry grin. "I didn't even realize I grabbed it. I have no idea why I did. Stupid." He shook his head, his blond hair, plastered to his face, dripping, making him look as though he were crying.

Gina took him by the elbow. "Paul, you go right into the bedroom and take a warm shower. I'm sure David can find something for you to wear. Meanwhile, I'll call Maryvale's sheriff's office and let them know about the bridge being out."

Twenty minutes later, Paul was dry, looking uncomfortably Yuppie-like in a pair of David's twill slacks and a mauve dress shirt. The slacks had had to be rolled up at the hem, and they were a bit snug at Paul's waist, but they were dry. He padded around in a pair of mauve socks. His strained expression told Gina and David that he'd never worn mauve and he'd be damned if he ever would again. David tried not to be amused. After all, Paul had had a rough time of it.

Gina had taken the sodden sack into the kitchen and retrieved the litter, the cat box, and put away the cat food. All that was left on the counter was the piece to repair the oven.

When Paul entered the kitchen, she smiled at him, remarking, "I can't believe you grabbed this sack as you were saving yourself."

Paul blushed furiously at her compliment. "Guess it's a holdover from my high school football days. You know, snag the pass and then make a dive for the goal."

Gina laughed gaily. Behind Paul, David scowled as she declared, "You were a quarterback? I always had terrible crushes on my high school's quarterbacks."

David's scowl deepened. Not only had he never been a quarterback, he'd never even gone to a school with a football team. Even today, he was at a loss when football was being discussed.

"What would you like for dinner, Paul, since you're the guest of honor—hero of the day, so to speak."

Paul grinned shyly. "Oh, I'm no hero."

"Oh, yes, you are," Gina countered, motioning toward where Lumper was heading—to the corner where the litter box had been set up. "Need I say more?"

This time Paul chuckled. It had a far too intimate and satisfied ring to it for David's taste. He cleared his throat, "Where's that oven part, Paul? I'll get it fixed and we can have baked fish."

Gina looked a little surprised. "You're going to fix the oven, David?"

He pinned her with a severe gaze. "Why not? I'm a physicist."

She smirked. "I don't think the job requires altering the oven's atomic makeup. Paul was given instructions, let him do it."

"Don't you think I can handle a simple job like this?"

She stared at him for a moment before she shrugged with indifference. "Okay, go ahead and try—just promise to pay for the part if another one has to be ordered. And that goes for the whole oven, if you ruin it."

"I'll help," Paul offered unenthusiastically.

"Don't bother," Gina protested, taking him by the arm. "Let's go listen to the weather report. Maybe they'll say something about how long it will take to repair Mason's Bridge."

"What did the sheriff say?" David picked up the antenna-shaped piece of black metal with wires protruding from its narrowed end, and frowned at it.

"They can't even begin to repair it until the rain stops," Gina called back.

"Damn," David cursed below his breath. That probably meant Paul would be their guest for at least one night. God forbid that it be more. David only had three weeks left to win Gina back, and another man's presence would throw a monkey wrench into his plans.

As David fiddled with the oven, managing to get nothing much accomplished but skinning his knuckles, and losing the lighthouse's only screwdriver behind the refrigerator, he could hear Gina and Paul talking in confidential tones. David was suffering in Jealous Man's Hell—a hell he'd made for himself. Pride had shoved him into trying to show Gina how handy he was. But if, after ten years of marriage, she hadn't gotten an inkling about his handiness, or lack of it—as was becoming apparent as far as oven repair was concerned—then she never would! Stupid! Jealous! Arrogant! Idiot! That's all he was proving to her—that he was a stupid, jealous, arrogant idiot!

"How's it coming in there, Mr. Goodwrench?" Gina goaded from the door after ten minutes. "Fish about done?"

"Very funny," he muttered, pulling his head out of the oven. "Okay—so I can't fix ovens. I admit it."

Gina was grinning at him. "Now, there's a news bulletin." She motioned for Paul to come in. "Could you try it? I'm getting hungry."

Twenty minutes later, Paul had pulled out the oven, disconnected some wires, connected some others and replaced the oven. Once the electricity was back on, they tested it. Much to David's chagrin, it worked perfectly.

"That's great, Paul," Gina gushed, irking David.

"It was nothing," Paul insisted. "Clute wrote down every step for me. Otherwise I'd have been lost, too."

David couldn't help but think that having written instructions might have been a real help for him—had he known they were on the premises. Valiantly he resisted mentioning that.

"You're being modest," Gina protested.

He's being a jerk! David mused irritably. But he managed to ask in an easy, friendly manner, "How about those fish, now?"

"Good idea," Gina agreed. "Paul? What about you and me making a salad."

"Salad?" David queried, turning to look at her, his expression thunderstruck. "You don't eat salads."

She laughed. "I don't have to eat it. It's for Paul. He loves salads."

David, exasperated, turned back to the refrigerator, pulling from it the wrapped fish. "I'd hate myself if Paul didn't get his damned salad!" he muttered.

"What?" Paul asked as he crossed the center line to get the salad makings from the refrigerator.

David's smile was polite, if somewhat stiff. "I was just saying we ought to put some chocolate-covered mints in it. That way Gina might enjoy some salad, too."

Both Paul and Gina laughed at David's joke. Unfortunately, David wasn't in the mood to join them.

It was nearly midnight. Gina was uncomfortable about having to go to bed with David—albeit a divided bed—while Paul was there. She'd kept the men up playing Scrabble games until she wasn't alert enough to fathom how to come up with a word when all the letters she had left were *A* and *R* and there was a perfectly usable *C* on the board.

Paul stifled a yawn.

"Why don't we call it an evening?" David suggested exhaustedly. It was apparent why Gina had been urging them to play game after game. He'd gone along with her for a while, but it was getting ridiculous.

"Just one more?" Gina pleaded. "I feel a winning streak coming on."

Paul stifled another yawn, this time not quite so successfully. "No, thanks. I'm beat. I guess my dash on the bridge took a lot out of me."

Good. Bring it up again, Mr. Heroic Quarterback, David mused wearily. Gathering up the game pieces, he offered, "I'll get some bedding for you, Paul."

"Thanks." Paul stood and stretched.

"I'm afraid the sofa's a little lumpy. And not nearly long enough for you," Gina commented. "Why don't you share the bed with David?"

Her husband had just returned to the door, his arms full of sheets a pillow and blanket, when she made her offer. He froze to the spot. "Not likely, damn it!" he shot back.

Gina grimaced, hating his quick, harsh show of proprietorship. "Let's not air our dirty linen, David. Be reasonable."

He paced across the room and dumped the bedding on the sofa before he turned to confront her. "Have you forgotten your back?"

She had, for a moment. But was *that* his reason or did he just want Paul to see who "possessed" her? Her anger flaring, she suggested, "Well, why don't *you* sleep on the couch, and Paul and I can share the bed!"

As soon as the words came out of her mouth, she was horrified at herself. She hadn't meant that—hadn't meant it to come out the way it had. She bit her lip, wishing she could take it back.

Paul broke into a fit of embarrassed coughing.

David simply stared, his face suddenly drawn and severe.

"I—I shouldn't have said that," she admitted weakly. I meant—er..."

"Say," Paul interjected, taking up the bedding. "I'll just make myself a bedroll on the floor right here. I'll be fine."

"Oh—okay..." Gina cast him a grateful look. "See you in the morning...."

David, his teeth clamped together, managed a pained smile, nodded his good-night and went into the bedroom.

Gina followed, her feet leaden. She'd hurt David with that thoughtless remark. What was worse, the idea of sleeping with Paul had never entered her mind. Sure, she didn't plan to be married to David any longer than necessary, but she'd never intended to inflict deliberate pain on him by letting him think that she would prefer sleeping with other men!

Once she'd closed the bedroom door, she turned toward David, who was silently unbuttoning his shirt, his back toward her. "I—I'm sorry. I wasn't thinking when I said that."

He said nothing. There was no sound but for the incessant rain pounding on the roof.

"You do believe me, don't you? I would never intentionally embarrass or humiliate you."

Slowly, he shifted to confront her, and her breath caught harshly in her throat when she saw the misery that shimmered in his eyes.

6

GINA FLINCHED. She had never seen her husband so upset before, though he had quickly averted his gaze. Wondering about the wisdom of her actions, she moved to encircle his waist with her arms. David had a terrific need to be in control, and had many times manipulated her tender emotions to get his way. She didn't understand why he needed to dominate, and she wished he would be more open and honest about his feelings. But right now, she didn't believe he was being controlling. He was truly hurt and trying to hide it. Her heart constricting with guilt over her hasty words, she pressed her cheek to his chest, whispering. "David, I don't want to sleep with Paul. It never entered my mind. Please forget that stupid remark."

Her unexpected effort at comforting him had brought hope leaping into his soul, but he didn't dare touch her, pull her hard and carelessly against him, or sweep her up and carry her to the bed as he so wanted to do. He didn't dare move. Yet, he knew his traitorous heartbeat was revealing his longing for her.

Gina felt his quickened heartbeat, felt the evidence of his desire, but somehow she couldn't back away, couldn't retreat into the safety of her determination to leave him. Though she knew he wanted her, she was also aware that he was making no move to take her. For some odd reason, that bothered her as much as it comforted her. Being close to him, her face pressed against the reassuring mat of his

chest hair—his inviting, familiar and sensual scent—
something deep inside her resisted pulling away.

Instead, she clung to his solid torso, and her wayward
hands began to explore the strong, long-cherished con-
tours of his back. After an indulgent moment, she lifted
her gaze to his face, for it seemed that he had stopped
breathing. When their eyes met, his expression was confused, yet his eyes were bright with gentle yearning. She
couldn't stand it. Couldn't stand the sweet longing—not
his, and not hers. She couldn't stand the fact that she'd
wounded him. And foolish though it was, she couldn't
stand giving him hope and then dashing that hope. She
promised herself this would be the last time. One parting
interlude in his arms. Her voice an emotion-roughened
whisper, she said, "There's a crazy part of me that will always love you—no matter what. If you want to make love
to me tonight—" she paused, her smile faint and reticent
"—then it's all right with me."

His eyes were suddenly masked by lowered lashes, but
his gaze drifted over her face for a long, silent moment.
With deliberate movements, he took hold of her arms and
slid from her embrace. Gina wasn't even wholly aware of
what had happened until he had stepped away from her,
and she felt the coolness of his absence. His expression had
gone from gentle and hopeful to harsh, almost distaste-
ful.

"Don't do me any favors," he whispered. "Unless you
want to come back to me, don't throw me sexual crumbs."
With that, he left her, retreating to his side of the bed,
which was hidden behind the hanging blanket. She could
hear buttons fly as he literally tore his shirt from his body.
There was a muffled thud as his trousers hit a wall, and
then she saw the bed shudder as he dropped heavily onto
it.

She felt sick to her stomach, left standing there alone, frustrated and confused. As the rain howled its scorn, she slowly regained the ability to move. Slumping dejectedly, she allowed a forlorn tear to slide down her cheek and she smiled tiredly. So, this was how it felt to be rejected? It was like a kind of death.

MORNING CAME with the detonation of heaven-splitting thunder. Gina woke abruptly from a bad dream. Shaking the sleep from her eyes, she realized her dream had stemmed from David's rejection last night—something she'd brought on herself. In her dream, he had continued to reject her, running from her, flying away, even disintegrating into thin air. Feeling oddly fatigued, she decided it would be wise to forget the night and face the day. When she sat up, it struck her that any dream where David was *leaving* her should be refreshing and—good. She frowned at the irony.

Movement caught her eye and she noticed that Lumper's backside and abbreviated tail protruded from the blanket that divided the bed. Seeking small comfort, she stroked his shank. He stretched, stood and disappeared beneath the divider, deserting her. "So, you're rejecting me, too," she mumbled sleepily. "Okay. You men stick together if you must. See if I care!"

Throwing back the covers, she went to the bathroom and flung the door wide only to be confronted by David's glistening nudity. With the storm raging outside, she hadn't realized he was even up, let alone just stepping from the shower. They both seemed riveted by the unexpectedly intimate encounter. David—captured in the process of drying his broad chest—stared at her, and she couldn't bring herself to do more than stare back at his tawny perfection.

After a tense minute, impatience showed in his cool gray eyes as he taunted, "To what do I owe this visit? More offers of charity sex?"

She blanched at his severe tone. "I—I had no idea you weren't in bed."

Draping his towel modestly about his waist, he made a sweeping gesture with his arm. "I was just leaving. Be my guest."

"I—will," she murmured tightly. "I—uh— Would you mind telling Paul I'll only be a few minutes. Then the bathroom is his."

David's slow grin was singularly unpleasant as he inquired, "Are you sure you don't want me to go get him now?"

His insult stung, and she retorted coldly, "If you must repay me for humiliating you by humiliating me, then go ahead."

A flash of self-contempt marred his features, and he mouthed a curse. Raking his hand through his damp hair, he wheeled away and slammed the door. The earsplitting noise it made was cloaked by the crash of nearby thunder.

David Baron, Gina's calm, reasonable professor-scholar-husband, had just hurled a door shut. And he'd done it hard enough to open the medicine chest, dislodge a bottle of aspirin and send it flying to the floor. The lid, not on solidly, bounced across the room to land at Gina's feet, and what seemed like thousands of little white pellets began dancing and skidding across the white tiles. Miserable, Gina lowered herself to sit on the edge of the tub and watched as the aspirins spun and hopped to a gradual halt. When the tablets had finally stilled, a tottering bottle of cologne crashed into the sink and shattered, permeating the tiny room with an overpowering, spicy scent.

She shook her head. David was really angry—violent enough to have killed a bottle of aspirin and a jug of Concealed Weapon. Sighing, she grabbed a towel and began to clean up the mess. As she wiped the swampy mess into a pile, she began to wonder at her solid, unruffable husband. He had a savage, unguarded side she'd never seen before. Where had it come from? Not even when a drunk had slammed into the side of his new BMW coupe had David even raised his voice.

With a concerned quirk of her brows, she realized she must be driving him right to the edge of sanity with this divorce business. But to violence? There was something frightening about this new fierceness he was revealing. But even more, there was something intriguing about knowing just how imperfectly human David could be. It was bewildering to discover so late in their marriage that *she* had the power to bring out such raw honesty in him. And, God help her, she didn't believe that could be all bad. If David had allowed her a glimpse of this fragile, mortal side earlier, then maybe, just maybe, their marriage might have been salvageable. But it was too late, now. She wiped away a futile tear, mumbling, "Far too late . . ."

THE DAY WAS PROGRESSING in a sodden, bleak fashion as far as David was concerned. He'd begun the morning with a fit of uncharacteristic jealous anger, and he was ashamed of himself. Anger and jealousy were such self-destructive emotions. He hated himself for wallowing in either. But he was equally ashamed of the way he was reacting to Gina's casual conversation with Paul. Casting them a furtive glance over the rims of his spectacles, he watched as Paul helped Gina organize her research papers.

Though he turned away, determined to ignore them, every so often he was drawn away from his physics journal by Gina's lilting laughter. He had to fight the urge to crumple the periodical in his fists. Gina was not being very professional—at least, not to his way of thinking. Giggling was not a prerequisite for writing a book. He'd written three, and he hadn't let out a chortle during the whole damned process.

And was batting her lashes at that—that blushing, inept Casanova at her side really necessary? It wasn't David's idea of the best method of shooting a literary project through to completion. On the contrary, it was more a way to titillate a man into throwing a brazen little tease on her back and smothering her with hot, moist—

He cleared his throat and irritably flipped to the next page, but chanced to look askance at his wife and find her moistening her lips—very slowly. He didn't know if she meant to be seductive with her tongue or if her lips were merely dry. Whatever the case, David was not a happy physicist.

"Oh, did I mention that the Maryvale Players are gearing up for our annual musical?" Paul asked as he straightened a stack of yellowing pages.

"I think you did. Tryouts are next Tuesday, aren't they?" Gina turned to face him.

"Tuesday night at seven in the community center."

"What musical are they going to do?"

"I don't know yet. We did *South Pacific* last year. So I can only guess it won't be that again." He handed her the stack. "Now, what do you want me to do?"

She gave him a handful of newspaper clippings. "Could you sort these by date—the most recent, last."

"Sure." He began to go through them. "Some of these are dated before the turn of the century."

Gina nodded, but didn't look up from her bulging file folder. "I know. I really must get them copied. There are a few that are in fragile shape."

"Gina?"

Paul's lovesick tone drew David's reluctant attention, but he pretended to read.

"Yes?" Gina looked up from her sorting.

"You're beautiful enough to play the lead—whatever musical they choose."

Gina blushed prettily. "You're such a flatterer, Paul."

She had the impertinence to slide a stealthy glance toward David, who immediately averted his gaze to stare stonily, unseeing at his periodical.

"No, I really mean it," Paul insisted.

"I don't know what to say," she demurred.

David pushed up from his chair, having had enough. "What about lunch?" he suggested a bit gruffly. "Anyone for a bowl of my leek-and-spinach soup?"

"David—give me a break," Gina began, her face pinched with distaste. "Leaky spinach?"

"Leek *and* spinach," David corrected from the kitchen door. "You know. Vegetables."

"Oh, those." She shook her head in mock distress. "I've heard they cause warts. I'd be careful."

He gave up and turned away.

"I am a little hungry, Paul. What do you say to a pastrami sandwich and a batch of fries on the side?"

"Uh—anything sounds good," Paul offered diplomatically. "Whatever you've got plenty of. I don't want to put you out."

Gina laid her work aside. "Don't be silly. We've got food enough for a couple of weeks of being stranded. Besides, it's not your fault the bridge washed out."

"Well, at least I can help."

"Slice up some pastrami, will you?" Gina asked as she began to rummage around in the refrigerator. David was already there, leaving her little space. "David, hand me that pastrami."

"You'd be better off with the spinach and leek—"

"Never mind," she retorted through a tired sigh. "Move over and I'll get it myself."

He retrieved the processed meat and handed it to her. "And fries?" he asked, sounding weary.

She eyed him irritably. "It's a vegetable."

"So are the potatoes growing on the abandoned plants near Chernobyl. Would you eat them?" Without waiting for an answer, he gathered up the bunch of fresh spinach, a tomato, and two large leeks, and moved away to drop them on his countertop.

He'd left so quickly, she didn't have time to think of an appropriate retort. How dare he compare indulging in a few French fries to a nuclear disaster! Instead, she vented her anger by plucking up the ingredients and retreating to her side of the kitchen. "Here." She thrust the pastrami at Paul and heard his pained exhale.

"Oh, I'm sorry, Paul," she declared, aghast. "My mind was on—something else."

With a feeble smile, he began to slice the meat.

David didn't bother to look over at her. Though he continued to chop his leeks, he was aware of exactly whom Gina had been wanting to hit when Paul suffered the pastrami to his solar plexus. It seemed a shame, but David wasn't cheered to know that young, blond and blushing Paul had suffered pain that had been meant for him.

THE RAIN RELINQUISHED its hold over the lighthouse just after darkness fell. The silence was almost deafening after so many hours of window-rattling squalls.

"Maybe they can start repairing Mason's Bridge to-morrow," Gina remarked as she looked up from her mail-order book, *The Dominating Male And How to Rid Yourself of Him.*

"Maybe," Paul echoed, dropping the paperback Gina had loaned him—a self-improvement manual that didn't appear to be his favorite kind of reading material. "Say," he inquired, "what are you reading, Gina?"

David glanced over from his easy chair where Lumper was sprawled in his lap. He announced impatiently, "It's one twisted woman's idea of how to emasculate men."

"Ha! Ha! Very droll, Dr. Baron," Gina countered before turning to Paul to explain. "Dr. Bella Von Bakker is an eminent psychiatrist, and her book has sold millions of copies—"

"And killed off a number of good marriages."

"*David,*" Gina retorted, shifting to pin him with a stern stare. "Do you mind? I'm trying to have a conversation over here."

Watching her solemnly, David didn't shrink from her haughty regard. A bitter smile fleetingly twisted his mouth. "Paul, the eminent Dr. Bella Von Bakker has been dubbed 'Dr. B. Breaker' by the American Psychiatrists' Association. She's a plague upon confused, discontented women." He shrugged and turned away. "Just thought you ought to know the other side of the story."

"She is not!" Gina groused. "I've never heard that—that B. Breaker thing. That's awful!"

He grunted. It sounded like sardonic laughter.

Gina slid closer to Paul and opened her book so that he could see. "Anyway, Paul, take chapter three, for in-stance—'Ladies, sharpen your machetes.'" She stopped and frowned. Somehow it did have a rather emasculating ring to it.

"I rest my case," David muttered, but he didn't look up from his reading material.

"Well," Gina defended, "take chapter four, then—'I'm gonna wash that jackass right outta my hair.'"

"Charming. A real healing message there," David countered, glancing over at them, one eyebrow lifted in an all-too-knowing expression.

Gina had had enough. She snapped the book closed and leaped up from the couch. "You think you know so damned much!" She started to rant on and then realized Paul would suffer. Instead, she suggested more quietly, "I think I'll fix myself a little snack. What about you, Paul? Chocolate sundaes sound good?" She took satisfaction in David's low groan.

The next morning the sun shone brightly, as though the twenty-four hours of scouring storms had polished it to a gleaming gold. Its warmth was invigorating, and at ten o'clock Gina decided to take a morning swim. Coming out of the bathroom, she tugged on the stretchy fabric of her bathing suit, remarking to herself, "This thing seems a little tight."

David came around from his side of the bed, wearing his jogging shorts. His eyes raked her body with bothersome thoroughness before he queried, "Could it be the chocolate sundaes?"

Her gaze snapped up to his face, both accusation and horror in her look. "No, it could not!" she denied vehemently. "This thing just shrank or something."

He inclined his head, looking doubtful. "Of course. Swimsuits are notorious for shrinking. My mistake."

She lifted her chin in a weak show of defiance, fearing he might be right. "I—I'm not gaining weight." She bit the inside of her cheek, but was forced to ask the dreaded question. "Am I?"

He seemed to take pity on her. Shaking his head, he murmured, "You look fine, but for your health's sake, you'd better—"

"Don't lecture me! Besides, I forgot. Now that I'm no longer The Dean's Wife—or soon won't be—I don't have to be a glowing example for young womanhood anymore!" she cried, whirling away. "Paul and I are going swimming. Enjoy your run!"

She hadn't sounded as though she cared if he went running or if he fed himself to sharks. When she'd slammed out of the bedroom, he looked down at the brown carpet and cursed his stupid need to remind her about her foolish life-style. *Damn!* All he wanted in the world was to love her the way she wanted to be loved. What in hell was the matter with him? Why couldn't he just have said, "Gina, get as chubby as you please. Just come back home with me. Be my wife. Love me the way you used to." Why couldn't he say that? Wasn't it in him to love her, no matter what? Was he so hidebound and health-conscious that he couldn't love her except in the image he'd fashioned for his mate—The Dean's Wife? And what exactly was his definition of The Dean's Wife, anyway? He began to mentally calculate: a spirited, intelligent woman with drive, wit, compassion . . .

He frowned, trying not to think about the fact that Gina was still all those things. Yet, she was far from his concept of what The Dean's Wife should be. So, what was the crucial difference—complete and total subservience? Is that what he wanted? Had he been selfish all these years, deluded into thinking he wasn't controlling like his father, when in reality, he was exactly like him? David felt himself physically shudder at the thought and shook his head. It couldn't be true. He'd fought so hard to be completely unlike the man.

Hell on earth was being caught in the vise of two op-
posing wills. Curse it! He wasn't like his father. He wanted
only the best for Gina. He loved her. For her own good,
he would persist until his will won out. Some nagging inner voice kept repeating, "For your own good, too. You
need her as much as she needs you."

He winced at the bald truth. He did need her. He needed
her sweetness, her tenderness, her wit—but dammit! She
really didn't want to gain weight. He'd seen it in her face.
He would persist. Their staying together was the best thing
for her—for them both—in the long run. Surely he could
make her see that.

He just hoped to hell that Paul wouldn't be their houseguest for much longer. He didn't know how much longer
he could take the man's fawning attentions to *his* wife! He
would hate to be driven to smashing the guy in the solar
plexus with a batch of leeks, or clouting him in the nose
with a hunk of tofu. He'd resorted to violence only once,
and he would never get over the gnawing guilt. Even so,
he had been feeling barbarous urges of late. He didn't like
to think he might follow through on one! Not again. He'd
made a promise to himself long ago.

ONCE OUT ON THE BEACH, Gina kept one eye on the lighthouse, expecting to see David follow her out, dogging her
heels. But he wasn't anywhere to be seen. Paul was coax-
ing her into the water, and she was hesitant. "Paul, I'm not
much of a swimmer."

"I'll teach you," he offered cheerily, obviously delighted to be separated from the scowling David.

"I don't know," Gina replied cautiously. "I'm—afraid
of things under the water."

Paul laughed, looking stocky in David's borrowed trunks. "There's nothing here that would hurt you," he assured.

She smiled faintly. "Promise? 'Cause, I really would like to be able to enjoy the beach."

He nodded and spread his arms in invitation. "I promise. Come on."

With a little squeal at the coolness of the water, she ventured out to Paul. They were thigh deep when he began to instruct her on the finer points of dealing with ocean tides and swells.

He took her hand, and they waded out deeper, until the surging sea was lapping below Gina's breasts. "Let's try the back float first. That way, you won't get your eyes in the salt water," Paul suggested. "But you probably ought to get some goggles and a snorkel to really enjoy the ocean."

"I'll think about it," she said, reluctance ripe in her tone.

"Lie back into my arms," he coaxed. "I won't let you go under."

After a brief deliberation, she pushed off the bottom and found herself bobbing around on the surface, with Paul's arms gently supporting her shoulders and thighs. She was a little embarrassed that he was touching her so intimately, but she tried to remember he was just teaching her to float on her back.

"Now what?" she rasped through clenched jaws.

"Relax," he cajoled with a grin. "You're doing fine."

She tried, but it was like trying to relax after being tossed from an airplane at twenty thousand feet. She remained stiff, and began to flounder.

Paul grabbed her to him as her mouth and nose went below the surface and, panicked, she began to choke. "You're okay, Gina," he assured softly. "I have you."

Frightened, she threw her arms about his neck, sputtering and coughing. When she'd regained her ability to breathe normally, she focused on Paul's face. He looked concerned. "Don't worry," she declared. "I'm going to live. I just don't know if I'll ever be able to relax, lying on my back in water. It doesn't seem like a very natural thing to do."

His face opened in a slow, relieved grin, and he confessed softly, "Gina—you know I'm crazy about you."

Before she had a chance to absorb his impulsive remark, he was lowering his lips to hers, kissing her with more heat than she would ever have imagined he could muster—especially since he was a guest in her own husband's house, or at least half her husband's house.

She found her wits belatedly, and pressed away, panting, "Paul—don't—please!"

His eyes were animated with his conquest, and there was raw lust in his expression. "Don't say that, Gina," he pleaded. "You know you and I could really have something going if it weren't for—you know. And he'll be gone soon. You said so yourself."

"But—" she pressed at his chest "—but—he isn't gone, Paul."

"Well, then let's give him a reason to go," he prompted, his eyes agleam with hunger. "You're such a great lady, Gina. I want you in my life."

Gina cast her gaze over Paul's shoulder, toward land. To her horror, she could see David standing high above them on the edge of the precipice. He looked remote, yet vulnerable, like some troubled man-god. In his coppery running shorts, he gave the illusion of nudity, but there was no illusion in the flawlessness that was embodied in his stance. His long legs were braced wide, exuding strength. The sun caressed his muscular torso, further enhancing the breadth of his shoulders. Though his arms were lowered to his sides, his hands were closed in tight fists. Every line of David's body gave off the message that he was holding himself in tight control.

Gina stared, and her heart gave an unhappy lurch. David was hurt—and furious.

7

"PAUL—ER— DAVID'S watching," Gina managed in an anguished whisper. "You'd better put me down."

Paul did a half turn and looked back over over his shoulder, his smile fading. "Oh, Lord," he moaned. "Well, I guess I asked for this. He looks pretty mad. Is he likely to get violent?"

Gina's gaze skittered back up to where David was standing. He looked so angry. If it had been anyone else, she would be sure that very soon, blood would be shed. But not David. He simply didn't have it in him. "Put me down, Paul," Gina repeated.

As soon as she'd slid back into the water, she began to trudge toward shore. But by the time she'd taken half a dozen steps, David had disappeared from view.

"Where are you going?" Paul called.

"To try to repair the damage."

"Why? Gina, isn't this going to work for you? Now that he sees you mean what you've been telling him, won't he leave?"

Gina peered back at Paul, whose expression was concerned. She suggested sadly, "And I could hit him over the head with a tire iron, too. That would be just as painful." She turned back toward shore and shouted so that he could hear: "I don't want to destroy him. I just want to leave him."

"All separations cause pain," Paul was protesting as he splashed through the surf to catch up with her. "David can't get beyond this without a little pain. Face it."

Gina shook her head. "A *little* pain isn't witnessing your wife making out with another man. That's a lot of pain."

"Well, hasn't he given you one hell of a lot of pain by coming out here and practically holding you hostage in your own home?"

She turned to squint up at Paul, pausing in the shallow water. "I—I suppose, in a way, he has. But you must understand—" She cleared her throat, cutting off a quaver in her voice that would reveal how close she was to tears. "The first time I saw him, David came into the bookstore where I worked, told me that we needed to go out to dinner because we ought to get to know each other. When I asked him why, he said, 'Because by next month at this time, you'll be my wife.'"

"The hell, you say," Paul interjected with disbelief.

"He said he was a man who got what he wanted. He—he's always been that way." Shaking her head sadly, she added, "That's our whole problem." She swallowed, remembering the uncharacteristic brashness of the handsome professor who'd entered her life and swept her so romantically into his. "Anyway—by the next month, we were married. He'd gotten his way—the first of many, many times."

"Why did you let him get away with it?" Paul groused.

She shrugged helplessly. "At first, it seemed so wonderful—to be so important to someone that he spent all his time thinking of me, doing for me. And besides, with David—" she lowered her head "—and with me, I suppose, it was love at first sight. We have a crazy sort of chemistry together. Even though his need to be in control drives me crazy, I refuse to be cruel to him."

"Are you sure he's not controlling you now, letting us see him up there?"

"He was on his way to jog, Paul," she retorted, not sure why she was defending him.

Paul took her by the arm, forcing her to meet his gaze. He was scowling. "Are you sure you *want* to leave the man? You don't sound very convinced of it, talking about him this way."

She avoided eye contact. "I'm sure I do. David insists on forcing me to fit a narrow little mold of his idea of the perfect wife, and I can't do it." Casting her gaze to heaven, she admitted, "I've quit trying and that's hard for him to accept. He's frustrated, mad . . ." With a sad, bitter laugh, she added, "Well, as mad as David gets—he went so far as to slam a door."

"Not exactly enough to call the cops with," Paul remarked, his expression annoyed.

"No. He's so polite and reasonable, I'm sure to the outside world he looks affectionate, and I come off as a flaming bitch. It's hard to point out anything blatant that he's done. It's just that I can't be a person in my own right as David's wife. It was partly my own fault," she admitted, clenching her fists. "I let him mold me into his idea of what a professor's wife ought to be—I led snobby charity drives, entertained boring people, smiled and obeyed until I'd had it up to my eyeballs." Her lips quivered with emotion. "I can't have children—my back injury prevents that—and I didn't have any driving urge to have a career. So, being naive and in love, I let him dictate my every move, my every thought, until he'd shaped me into the woman he wanted."

Paul took her by both arms, vowing low, "Damn it, Gina. You're exactly the woman I want, just as you are."

Wiping away a tear, she smiled at him, but it was a pitying smile. He saw it for what it was and reluctantly released her.

"Paul, I'm not ready for another man. I'm still married to David, and I haven't figured out how to rid myself of the baggage that relationship has me dragging around." She touched his cheek. "You're a wonderful person. Give me time. Okay?"

Paul's pinched expression eased a little, and he managed a halfhearted smile, too. "Okay." Motioning toward the lighthouse, he asked, "So, what do we do about Mr. Madder-than-Hell Manipulator?"

She cast her eyes in that direction and mused, "Oh, he won't get violent. But I think it would be better if you let me go up there alone."

"Are you sure?"

She laughed, but it was a melancholy sound without conviction. "I'm almost one-hundred-percent sure. But an hour ago I wouldn't have thought you were going to kiss me, either."

This time it was Paul's turn to laugh sadly. "An hour ago, neither did I. You were just so cute and helpless in the water..."

Gina shook her head at him. "Men. Why do you think 'cute and helpless' is so darned appealing?"

He gave her a sheepish look. "We're all macho brutes, I guess."

"Don't I know it," she grumbled. With a wave she added, "Wish me luck."

"Luck," he called. "How long do I have to stay out here?"

"Until you see me again."

"What if you're dead?"

Reluctant laughter gurgled in her throat. "Thanks for the vote of confidence."

When she entered the lighthouse, it was deathly still. There was no one to be seen but Lumper. He was asleep on David's chair, oblivious to any catastrophe that might be in the making.

She tried her voice, but her throat was so parched from nervousness that no sound would come. Swallowing, she tried again, "David?" It came out in a fearful squeak.

"In here, Gina," he called. The unexpected smoothness of his tone was as unsettling as thunderous rage would have been.

She crept uncertainly into the bedroom. When she rounded the bed's divider, David was sitting there, fully dressed, looking casually preppy—wire rimmed glasses and all—reading a book. He lifted his gaze when she appeared, his expression unreadable. "What can I do for you?"

She stared. "Are you all right?"

An eyebrow rose in question. "Why do you ask?"

She winced inwardly at his cat-and-mouse game. Preparing to be shredded by his biting intellect, she forced herself to ask, "What are you reading?"

He held up the book so that she could see that it was Dr. Bella Bakker's ill-famed denunciation of the male of the species. At her confused expression, he explained, "I just wanted to see if you learned that from her book."

"That?" Gina asked, feeling the hair prickle at her nape. *Here it comes.*

He inclined his head in the general direction of the beach. "That," he repeated solemnly. "Or did you come up with it on your own?"

"I—" Her legs too weak to hold her, she sank down to perch on the edge of the bed. "I didn't come up with it at all. Paul—well, I choked and he said I looked so cute and helpless that he . . ." Her voice failed her, and she found herself unable to do more than chew the inside of her cheek—and wait.

David merely watched her without speaking. But his nostrils flared, giving away his anger. When Gina could hardly bear the sizzling quiet any longer, he queried stonily, "He—what?"

Nerves wound taut, she confessed, "*Kissed* me, damn it! He kissed me. You know it! I know it! Go ahead and punch me. I know you want to! I'd rather you get it over in one swift blow than sit there and cross-examine me to death!"

With a cynical smile tugging at the corners of his lips, he asked, "What good would hitting you do?"

She hugged herself, feeling chilled more from his tone than the dampness of her bathing suit. "I—I don't know. Sometimes I think you're not even human, David. You're so controlled."

"Would you feel better if I hit you?"

"Don't be tedious," she cried, exasperated. "Men! You're all the same. You like your women cute and helpless and manageable and—and when we're not, you try to make us feel guilty about it!"

"Is that so?"

"Yes," she shouted defensively. "And another thing! You'd be happy if we spent our lives flat on our backs. You—Paul—all you lustful, self-centered men!"

He tossed the book to the floor and stood, stalking toward her. "I wouldn't talk if I were you, my lustful little siren. I've seen you flapping your lashes at Paul and sticking out your tongue invitingly. What the hell did you expect the man to do, slap your face?"

"Why—I never—"

His laughter was harsh. "Don't deny it. You were playing one of us against the other and you know it. Just what did you want? A fistfight? A duel, perhaps? Do you need to know men will fight over you even though you're turning a ghastly, aged thirty?"

She blinked, unconsciously retreating from him by leaning back on the bed. "I had no such thing in mind, David. You're twisting everything. You're acting like it was my fault!"

"Am I?"

He was towering over her now, straddling her legs with his own. "Yes!" she protested. "And you're wrong. It wasn't my fault. It wasn't anybody's fault—"

"What do you want from me, Gina?" he asked suddenly, his question a sharp, incisive query. "Do you want me to suffer?"

"No! I want you to leave!"

Taking off his glasses, he rubbed his eyes for a moment, letting out a long sigh. Tossing the glasses to the bed, he avowed, "I'm not going without you."

"I'm not going back, David," she declared in a hoarse whisper.

He bent over her, laying a hand on either side of her, preventing any escape. Forced back flat on the bed now, she grew alarmed, knowing her chance at flight had been blocked. She was staring up at him, wide-eyed, fearful that he was going to strangle the life out of her; his features were so tense, so savage. Not knowing what to do, she grasped him by his tie and bluffed wildly, "David, get off of me. Don't make me use force!"

When she tugged on his tie and cried out her idle threat, there was a flash of surprise across his face. Then, so suddenly as to startle Gina badly, David's features softened in a slow grin. An odd sort of challenge glittered in his eyes and he began to chuckle. "Physical violence, Gina?" he murmured in a thoroughly sexy drawl. "You frighten me." Lowering himself atop her, he whispered near her ear, "I'm paralyzed with fright. Say you won't hurt me."

"David . . ." she pleaded through a constricted breath. "You're—crushing me."

"What? I can't hear well when I'm paralyzed with fear," he taunted, his lips brushing her cheek.

"I—said—" She couldn't help it. She found herself grinning against her will. "Okay, you're a very funny man. Now get up or I really will have to hurt you." She was struggling now, but only playfully. "You're terrible." She couldn't contain a giggle. "David—honestly—I can't breathe."

"I'm too terrified to move, Gina. I hate being threatened with violence. It's so—vulgar."

"I'll show you vulgar!" She laughed, feeling strangely giddy. His breath on her ear felt so sensual, and his lips, grazing the sensitive lobe, made her spine tingle with delight. "If you don't get off me right now I'll be forced to toss you to the ground and place you in a hammerlock. Remember I took that self-defense course last summer."

"I think I'm going to faint," he said, his deep voice tinged with laughter.

"Oh, honestly!" she cried, provoked but laughing. "All right, you asked for it." With a mighty shove, she managed to roll him onto his side, toward the edge of the bed. What she didn't anticipate was that he would grab her, compelling her to roll with him. For an instant, they teetered on the edge and then they fell to the floor, where Gina landed on top of him, straddling his hips.

The trip down to the floor had been accompanied by a high-pitched wail. Gina had a feeling that the half laugh, half scream had emanated from her own lips, not David's so-called petrified ones. Once on the floor, she found herself nose to nose with her contrary husband. He was grinning up at her, holding her tightly. Gina berated herself. She was enjoying this far too much for her own good.

"You bully," he accused softly. "Now that you've thrown me to the floor, what are you going to do with me?"

She could feel his laughter all through her body. He was incorrigible, irresistible and thoroughly desirable! "David!" she retorted, her cheeks hot with indignation and an unwanted mixture of feelings that included a desire to kiss him—the *bum!* "I'm going to tweak your nose!" she warned, looking as stern as she could manage. "You hate it when I tweak your nose."

"Getting kinky, are we?" he chided. "Tweak away, honey, but beware of what I tweak in return."

She took his dare and reached up to grab his nose, but before she could, he caught her wrist. A full-fledged wrestling match ensued, filling the room with playful squeals and full-bodied laughter.

When they became aware that they were no longer alone in the room, Gina had David half out of his shirt, and his tie was stuffed partway down the bodice of her bathing suit.

Paul cleared his throat and was backing out of the room he'd just burst into, when Gina jumped up. Straightening herself, she blanched to realize that David's tie dangled incriminatingly from between her breasts.

"Good grief, Gina," Paul sputtered, "I heard your screams. I—I guess I thought you needed—help. . . ." He swallowed, his face beet-red with embarrassment.

David sat up and leaned back against the bed, his eyes glittering with amusement at her expense. Drawing up a knee, he casually began to button his shirt as he asked, "Do you need any help, Gina?"

She could only shake her head, humiliation heating the skin of her face. "If you guys will excuse me, I think I'll go into the bathroom and stay there until I die."

Fighting a grin, David asked, "Could I have my tie back?"

She shot him a murderous look, yanked the tie from its intimate captivity and tossed it at him.

Adjusting it about his neck, he offered, "I'll send you in a little leek-and-spinach soup from time to time."

"That ought to finish me off," she mumbled, slinking miserably away.

When the door to the bathroom clattered shut, the men eyed each other for a long, silent moment. All the humor vanished from David's expression, his lustrous silver eyes going leaden.

The crimson color of Paul's face didn't diminish, but his anxiety-riddled frown deepened. "Well, Baron," he began haltingly, "I suppose you want to punch me." Swallowing hard, he groused, "Okay, man, I'll fight you for her."

David pursed his lips. His eyes, now cool and distant, raked Paul's stocky body and worried face. After a palpable moment, when David decided the younger man might have a stroke if he didn't say something, he asked, "Which would you prefer, Page, pistols at fifty paces—or, perhaps, tuna-and-bean salad in tomato shells?"

Paul had opened his mouth, but no words came when David's question sank in. He stood there, his lips gaping in shock.

"Well?" David prodded, his tone sardonic.

Paul's lips opened in a weak smile. "Uh—salad—I guess. Thanks, man."

"Salad, it is," he acknowledged with a curt nod. Standing, he arched his spine and stretched his shoulders. "You can scoop out the tomato pulp."

Paul nodded dumbly, still looking perplexed. "Uh—sure. No problem."

As David headed toward the bedroom door, Paul halted him with a tentative hand on his arm. "Look, Baron, I want to apologize for what I did. I hope Gina told you it wasn't her fault. It was entirely my idea."

David turned to face the younger man. "I know that." His voice grew ominously quiet as he added, "Paul, I'm going to be frank with you. As God is my witness, I was hard-pressed not to . . ." He paused, flexing his fists in agitation for a moment before he regained his composure. Cocking his head toward the kitchen, he finished quietly, "Let's get lunch."

Heaving a timorous sigh, Paul nodded.

The bathroom door opened and Gina appeared, dressed in a terry robe, her hair wrapped in a towel. Looking contrite, she asked, "Is it lunchtime?"

David regarded her wryly as he leaned against the doorjamb. "Are you dead already?"

She shrugged. "I'll die later. Right now, I'm starved." She managed a sick smile. "Everything all right?"

Paul cast a quick glance toward David for encouragement.

"Everything's fine," David assured them both. But there was a hard, unfamiliar sheen in his eyes.

She clasped her hands before her for want of any better thing to do with them. "Paul? How about me frying us up a batch of chicken?"

Paul looked uneasy. "I think I'll have salad with David. Actually my stomach can't take too much greasy food," he admitted, his gaze plummeting to his feet.

She grimaced, unable to tell if that was the truth or if Paul had decided to appease David. She was put out with him for deserting her team. Surely Paul wasn't afraid of David! Though Paul wasn't as tall, he was stockier and younger.

Still, although Paul might not believe it, David was a fraud as far as becoming violent was concerned. She'd never seen him do more than flare his nostrils at a person, let alone hit one. Irritated, she planted her hands on her hips and admonished, "You two are jellyfish, that's what you are."

"But health-conscious jellyfish," David corrected, turning toward the kitchen. "Why don't you change and then join me in the kitchen, brother jellyfish," he suggested over his shoulder.

"Be a minute," Paul called back. Passing Gina one last, forlorn look, he disappeared into the bathroom.

WHEN GINA HEARD the shower running, she decided she'd better hurry and dress if she didn't want Paul to step out of the bathroom and catch her in her underwear. Rushing to change, she opted to continue to wear her bra—especially considering what had happened in the ocean. *That* had come out of the blue.

She donned an oversize fluorescent orange T-shirt and a faded-black pair of baggy sweatpants. She had no intention of sexually arousing either of the horny men she was having to contend with! As she combed through her hair, she found herself thinking about David—and Paul. What would she have done if they'd gotten into a fight over her? She hoped she would be appalled. She should be happy they had settled their differences in an adult, nonviolent way. So, why was she feeling so depressed? Would she have wanted David to haul off and smash Paul in the teeth, defending her honor? What sort of man did she want, anyway? An immature thug? Or, maybe just a human being?

Barefoot, and with worries nagging her, she ambled out to the kitchen so that Paul would have privacy to dress. David was mixing something in a bowl. Four tomatoes were sitting on the counter beside him. She didn't speak as she rummaged through the refrigerator, looking for her package of chicken legs—the only part of a chicken she could abide.

David continued to stir, not acknowledging her. She had to get on his side of the kitchen to cook the chicken, so she decided to proceed without asking his permission. After dumping a heaping cup of shortening into a skillet, she stepped back across to her own side. With nothing to do but wait until the shortening was melted, she leaned against the sink, watching David's tensed back as he worked.

A thought kept nagging her and she decided she had to know the answer, even if it meant speaking to David. She cleared her throat. "What would it take to make you mad enough to hit someone?"

He stopped stirring and passed her a dubious glance over his shoulder. "You mean some poor slob like Paul?"

She shook her head. "No. I mean—like, anyone?"

He turned to face her, his expression closed, leaning back against the countertop, too. They looked like a couple of very serious bookends. He took in her attire and shook his head. "Why are you dressed like a Halloween pumpkin?"

"Because I *feel* like it," she observed dryly. "Answer my question."

He allowed a broad shoulder to rise and fall. "I won't hit anyone, Gina. Not for any reason."

"Not even if he was trying to kill me?" she blurted, stunned.

He half smiled. "You're the self-defense expert. What could I do that you couldn't?"

She sniffed scornfully. "You could crush him when you fainted."

Crossing his arms, he grew serious again. "If someone were trying to kill you, I would do my best to defend you. I'm not sure that hitting the culprit would be wise. I'd have to know the exact scenario."

She groaned melodramatically. "Oh, there's just no impulsiveness in you at all, is there!"

His solemn eyes searched her face. "Not as far as violence goes. I don't care to dwell on the subject."

"Well, dwell on it for a minute."

His frown deepened. "Why?"

"Oh, never mind. You're hopeless!" It occurred to her that because of her mental turmoil she'd forgotten to make her special secret batter to coat her chicken. Shaking her head at David, she began to gather ingredients.

"What are you looking for in a man, Gina? Do you want someone who breaks legs for the mob?"

With her arms full of prepackaged pancake batter, eggs, cream and salt, she twirled around to eye him with ill temper. "I don't know a single woman in the world who would ask her husband if he'd hit a man to save her life and have that man reply that he'd have to know the entire scenario, David. I give up!"

She dumped her supplies on the counter and turned her back on him.

"Would you have been happy if Paul and I had bloodied each other's noses over you?"

"Forget it!" she spat, dumping pancake batter into a mixing bowl.

"We still could, you know. I'll go get him and we can mix it up a little before lunch. Would that satisfy your blood-lust?" Under his breath, he muttered, "What do you want to be, Helen of Troy?"

She dropped the pancake-batter box with a loud *thunk* that lifted a cloud of flour into the air. Coughing, she spun to confront him again, declaring, "Leave it alone. I don't want a thing. Especially from you. I was wondering if you had any spirit in you at all. Are you made of blood and bone or—cold, sterile computer chips?"

Wounded by her suggestion that he was without all the passion allowable to any one human being, he asked darkly, "You can say that to me? After what we've shared?"

She colored, even beneath the dusting of flour that covered her face. "We weren't discussing our sex life."

"Speaking of that," he cut in, "what do you suppose would have happened in that bedroom if Paul hadn't blundered in?"

She pulled her lips between her teeth, tasting the batter and grimacing, but more at the disturbing memory than the doughy flavor. They both knew what would have happened on that bedroom floor. She turned away and pressed her hands on the countertop, feeling dejected. Weak! Weak and stupid, that was what she was. Fighting for control, she managed tiredly, "Nothing would have happened." It was a bitter lie, but she was so over-wrought, she couldn't deal with the truth. In self-defense, she embellished on the lie. "I'm over you, David. You're inflexible and manipulative. Why can't you just go back to Boston?"

"Possibly because I'm inflexible and manipulative," he growled.

She sagged further, moaning tiredly, "Oh—hell . . ."

"Gina—"

"What!" she cried, spinning back, completely at the end of her emotional rope. "What momentous, earth-shattering revelation must you relate to me now? Do enlighten me! I doubt if I can go on one more instant without the genius of your verbosity! Go ahead! *Dazzle me with your brilliant insights, damn you!"*

Her gaze shot across the space, hit his, and was gripped as if in a vise. His taut stance gave her nothing, but the torment in his eyes was debilitating. "I just thought you should know," he began, his lips curling sardonically, "that your grease is burning."

Her eyes widened and she scurried to douse the flaming mess by dumping the bowl of batter over it. With the fire successfully smothered, Gina's mind was freed to sense a hideous, gnawing guilt about how she'd just treated David. She'd been rude and unfair. When she turned to apologize, she was startled to find that he had gone.

8

THEN SHE HEARD IT. The phone was ringing. Gina rushed to the kitchen door in time to see David pick up the receiver. Leaning against the doorjamb, she wondered who might be calling. Maybe there was some news about the bridge.

"Why, hello, Quentin," David began, and Gina suddenly felt sick. "What a surprise," David was saying. "The connection is quite good. Oh? You're not in Boston? Los Angeles?" He turned to face Gina and frowned at her obvious distaste before he added, "Of course, we'd love to have you drop by. When?"

Gina was making a sour face and shaking her head. There could be no mistaking the fact that she didn't want Quentin Finchkelp to visit them. All she needed was the president of Albert Einstein Institute and Estelle, his dull wife, to drop by. She shook a warning fist at David, who was assuring Quentin, "We'd be delighted."

"The bridge is out," she hissed under her breath. "They can't get here."

"Next Wednesday would be wonderful. We'll expect you for dinner."

Gina's hopes were dashed. The sheriff's office had told them the bridge would be repaired, or at least, crossable, by Monday. She pantomimed a gag by sticking her finger in her open mouth.

David shook his head at her as he spoke into the phone. "Gina is right here. Yes, Quentin, tell Estelle she's ecstatic."

Gina dramatized being hanged, sticking her tongue out and crossing her eyes.

Paul, who had come out of the bedroom—showered and dressed in a pair of David's brown slacks and a brown sweater—burst out laughing at Gina's antics.

David grimaced. "Laughter, Quentin? Yes, that was our houseguest. He was—er—reading a particularly humorous anecdote in *Business Week*. Yes. It is a witty magazine."

Paul had gotten himself under control, but Gina was making it difficult. She'd armed herself with wads of newspaper and was flinging them at David as he talked.

Batting them away, David eyed her with dark admonition, but his voice was all charm. "Certainly, Quentin. I believe I do recall Estelle's lactose intolerance—and her allergy to strawberries. We'll look forward to seeing you then."

When he hung up, Gina let out a groan. "David, how could you invite Prune Face and Watermelon Butt here? This is *my* home. I left that world behind when I left you!"

"What was I supposed to say? 'No, I realize you traveled three thousand miles, but my mutinous wife is gagging and pelting me with spitwads at the very idea of seeing you?'"

"Yes, that's exactly what I wanted you to say."

His narrowed gaze raked her face, and he growled, "Gina, you must—"

The ringing of the phone interrupted him. Picking it up, he controlled his voice and said, "Yes?" After a moment, his grim expression softened and he smiled.

Gina grew suspicious, asiding to Paul, "I hope that's a message that Quentin and Estelle have changed their minds about coming to dinner and have decided to join a lactose-scorning religious cult somewhere."

Paul grinned at her, but said nothing.

"That's good news, Sheriff. I'll tell Paul." When he hung up, he glanced at the younger man, his expression pleased. "They've got a temporary support across Mason's Gulch. The sheriff said if you can get over there this afternoon, the construction crew can get you across. And we can get to town for supplies."

Paul's grin faltered. Nodding, he said, "If one of you could give me a ride?"

Gina took his arm and aimed him toward the kitchen. "We've got plenty of time, Paul. Have lunch first. How about *baked* chicken?"

"Well . . ." He cast an apprehensive glance over his shoulder in time to see a frigidness invade David's eyes. "Uh—maybe just a quick bite."

AFTER PAUL LEFT on Sunday afternoon, the rest of that day was spent in tense silence, as was Monday and most of Tuesday. Gina tried to lose herself in working on her book. David, she noticed unhappily, once again became his unflappable self, either jogging, reading or working on what she guessed to be another in a long line of scholarly physics papers. It angered her that he was so stubbornly bent on remaining with her, attempting to wear her down, no matter how thoroughly she tried to ignore him.

Tonight, she vowed, she was going to get out of the house and be free of her husband's silent coercion. She was going in to Maryvale to try out for their musical. She didn't even care what it was, as long as it got her away from David and involved in her new life and her new town.

She'd show him that he was wasting his time, staying here. Becoming a part of the Maryvale community was going to be a fresh start for her. She was determined to get on with her life in spite of David Baron!

At six o'clock, she flounced out of the bedroom wearing a battered Panama hat, a huge, striped turtleneck knotted at one hip, baggy twill trousers rolled up to mid-calf and Madras espadrille. She expected to draw a condemning remark from David—or, at least, that had been her plan. But when she whirled about to confront him, he wasn't in his regular chair.

"David?" she called, wondering if he was in the kitchen. Her only answer was a curious meow from Lumper, who was coming around the corner.

Shrugging, Gina slipped on her sunglasses. "Too bad. He'd have hated this outfit." With a disappointed sigh, she left, not wanting to be late for the tryouts. Feeling as though she looked terribly "show biz," Gina decided there wasn't an ounce of stodgy Dean's Wife left in her anywhere! She had a feeling that being in this musical was going to be a vastly liberating experience for her.

It surprised her to notice that David's rented Mercedes wasn't in the gravel parking area behind the lighthouse. He'd probably run out of wheat germ or something just as boring. She only hoped she didn't meet him along the road; she didn't care to become involved in a debate about her trying out for the Maryvale Players' musical. David's idea of entertainment was a reading of *The Canterbury Tales*, tediously recited in Middle English.

Tryouts were being held in the community-activity center, located in the back section of Maryvale's immense library. When Gina pulled up, she was surprised to see the lot teeming with cars. She'd had no idea what a big event Maryvale's musicals were.

Suddenly nervous, she walked into the old stone building and followed the hand-painted signs, taped up along the dank corridor. They read Tryouts This Way, and were accompanied by directional arrows.

By the time she got to the second floor, she could hear the din of laughing voices and knew she must be close. Her heart hammered with anxiety. She hadn't been in an amateur production since she was in high school. Her school, in rural Massachusetts, hadn't been very big. She'd been the lead, but who knew how much of an honor that was in a school with only three hundred pupils—and a scant thirty students in the drama club?

She shrugged off her fear. After all, this was a community project, not the dawning of a theatrical career. Just being a part of it would be fun, even if she ended up cleaning paintbrushes.

A friendly-looking man with bushy eyebrows and a shock of lead-gray hair greeted her at the door. Introducing himself as Freddy Potter, local mortician and play director, he handed her a name tag and told her to "mill around and mingle." Tryouts for *Oklahoma* would begin in twenty minutes.

So the play would be *Oklahoma*. Gina was thrilled. She'd always liked that musical. And she loved Westerns. This was really going to be fun!

A short while later, she saw the Norwells who owned the grocery store and the Vladimirs who ran the drugstore and soda fountain. Paul found her and pointed out Iduna Brand, who owned the beauty parlor, and Norris Costby, the bank's only teller. There were other familiar faces, too, and soon Gina felt at ease—at least for a while.

After noticing several times that a burly redheaded man seemed to be staring at her from across the room, she nudged Paul and indicated the stranger with an inconspicuous nod. "Who's that?" she whispered. "He looks kind of familiar, but I can't place him."

"Oh, Max?" He shook his head. "He works for American Parcel Delivery. If you've ever ordered anything by mail, most likely Max has del—"

"Oh, good grief!" she cried under her breath, recalling vividly when and where she'd seen him before. She'd been naked!

"Say, what's the matter, Gina?" Paul asked. "You went pale, just then."

"Oh, nothing. Forget it." Grimacing, she toyed with her hat brim, lowering it farther across her brow. But she was sure, by the crooked grin he'd been directing her way, that he recalled who she was and how they'd almost met.

"Well, what I was about to tell you before was that Iduna has played the lead the last four years," Paul whispered as they took their seats for the beginning of tryouts. "But I think you're much prettier."

Gina shook her head at him, her eyes on Iduna. Her sleek black hair was pulled back into a long French braid. "She's lovely. And I bet she sings like a bird."

Paul nodded. "Pretty good—except when she has to go for a real high note. Then—" he made a face "—cover your ears. But she's the best we've had in Maryvale."

"Hi there," came a cigarette-rough voice from behind Gina. She felt a tap on her shoulder and turned, curious, then blanched. It was Max, leering openly at her from the row behind.

She tried to look pleasant—pleasant but not interested. "Hello," she offered without much enthusiasm.

"Remember me?" he asked, his leer perfectly vile.

Paul had turned now, but he said nothing as Gina nodded vaguely. "I do, but I'd appreciate it if you don't mention it again."

He chuckled and winked. "Our little secret, honey."

Gina's face went hot. Obviously this Max person had gotten the wrong idea about her. Apparently he believed that just because a woman prances around outside naked, she was loose or something. Try as she would, she couldn't really blame him for that.

"Say, Max," Paul inquired. "You know Gina?"

He chuckled again. It was a depraved sound that made Gina feel like she needed a shower. "Yeah, we met once." His slitted gaze shifted to Gina as he added, "Didn't we, honey?"

Paul frowned.

Gina cleared her throat. "Look, if you don't mind, I'd appreciate it if you wouldn't call me that."

Still smiling, he ran a thick paw along his temple, as if smoothing his mane of hair, though Gina could tell it was heavily moussed into place and probably couldn't be destroyed by a tidal wave. "Then maybe you'd better tell me your name," he suggested smoothly. "I'm Max Murphy. Any time I'm out your way making deliveries, don't hesitate to ask me to stop by and do you any little—favor."

"Uh—Max, this is Gina Baron," Paul interjected. "She's getting a divorce."

Gina spun to eye Paul narrowly. "Thanks for the help," she retorted thinly.

Paul looked confused. "What's with you and Max?" he asked. But before Gina could reply, Fred Potter called for quiet and explained that the lead characters would be decided tonight. Tomorrow he'd announce the supporting cast and stagehands.

"He'll have to telephone me," Gina whispered. "I'll be entertaining David's boss."

Paul lifted a skeptical brow. "Are you going to be a good girl?"

With a defiant smirk, she asked, "What do you think?"

Paul grinned and shook his head, but they didn't have time to say more. Tryouts had begun.

When her name was called, Gina stood to go but was stopped by a paw on her wrist. "I'll be rooting for you, pretty lady," Max whispered from behind her.

"Me, too," Paul promised, smiling encouragingly.

Trying not to think about the fact that Max Murphy would be envisioning her naked, she moved on rubbery legs to the stage.

The pianist was a sprightly octogenarian named Marjorie. She was a wonderful musician and could improvise just about anything anyone wanted to sing. Gina hadn't thought about having to prepare something, so her mind raced as she tried to decide what might best showcase her voice. When Fred greeted her with an encouraging pat on the shoulder and asked the dreaded question, she managed to squeak out, "Does Marjorie know 'The Indian Love Call'? It's from an old Jeanette McDonald and Nelson Eddy movie."

Marjorie nodded and her sharp blue eyes twinkled merrily. Apparently she preferred the old songs to some of the contemporary stuff she'd been asked to play. Moments ago, Idi had managed to pull off a passable version of Madonna's latest hit. More than half the credit should rightfully have gone to Marjorie, who'd done a miraculous rendition at the piano.

"'Indian Love Call' is fine," Fred agreed. "But who do you want to sing it with you? It's a duet."

She fiddled nervously with her hat brim. That hadn't occurred to her. "Well, er, I—"

"How about me?" came a strong baritone voice from the rear of the room. Gina jumped at the familiar sound and her gaze shot back to see David ambling up the center isle.

Her eyes widened at the sight, for he looked nothing like the Yuppie professor she'd married. He sported a pair of faded jeans that hid little of his masculine attributes, glossy black cowboy boots and a flannel shirt, its sleeves rolled up to reveal muscular forearms. To top off the ensemble, he wore a black cowboy hat. Its wide brim was pulled low, obscuring his eyes in shadow—but not his strong jaw or his appealing half-smile.

There was an appreciative buzzing among the feminine members of the Maryvale Players as this tall, broad-shouldered cowboy made his way to the front of the room. Then, to Gina's utter astonishment, he placed one hand on the stage and pushed himself up over the top and righted himself, as though he'd leaped across fences and onto broncos' backs all his life.

Thrusting out a hand to Fred, he drawled, "Howdy, I'm Dave Baron. I'll sing with the little lady." The words had come out in a flawless Texas accent, devoid of the clipped British intonation he'd acquired while living in England. All at once Dr. David Baron of London and Boston was every inch a Texan! Gina's lips dropped open in shock.

Fred was grinning broadly. "Glad to meet you, Dave," he said, pumping the taller man's hand. Then his face took on a curious note of recognition. "Baron, you say?"

David glanced at Gina as he said, "Right."

"Oh, Gina's husband," Fred mused aloud. "Well—welcome to tryouts, Dave. I guess you're here for a while?"

Gina winced. Though she'd tried to keep David and his reason for being here a secret, the news had obviously gotten around.

"I'm visiting for the summer," David was saying. "I hope it's okay if I try out."

Fred nodded. "All we ask is that you sing loud and, if you get a lead part, don't run out on us before opening night."

David nodded. "You've got a deal."

What is his game? Gina cried mentally. Did he plan to keep her his prisoner even in *town?*

When she cast him an incredulous look, he snagged her gaze and held it with those shadowed eyes, and as Fred moved away to leave the couple alone at center stage, he whispered, "I would have preferred Verdi's *Aïda,* darling, but in a pinch, I can dredge up my country-boy past."

"You don't know this song!" she retorted under her breath.

"I've heard those old seventy-eights your grandmother left you for years. I imagine I could sing everything Jeanette and Eddy ever recorded in my sleep."

"Please—I don't want you here," she sputtered, upset.

His lips twisted devilishly as he mouthed, "I know."

Gina saw no laughter in his eyes, and she felt sick. When bent on getting his way, David was a hard man to oppose.

Marjorie began her musical introduction. David turned to half face the audience, and, getting into character for the love song, placed a caressing arm about Gina's shoulders. Just before she was to begin her part of the haunting lyric, he whispered, "I hope those aren't my good pants."

She looked up at him lovingly, as was required by the song, and murmured, "They are. And if you like this outfit, just wait until tomorrow night."

The music paused and then swelled. It was time for Gina to start. Her smile, as she began to sing, had more to do with his grimace than the obligatory loving expression. Her face lifted sweetly upward as she expressed her undying love for her Indian brave.

David answered, his voice gentle yet strong, and as lush as any male singer Gina had ever heard. When their parts required that they blend their voices, he even harmonized perfectly with her melody.

The song ended, and their vocals drifted away on a lingering seductive note. For a long moment there was no sound at all in the room. Then, all at once, the onlookers burst into applause. Some of the most appreciative stood and whistled.

Fred bounded up the stage steps to congratulate them for an awe-inspiring performance.

Shaking David's hand, he smiled at Gina and declared, "If you two can act at all I think I've found my Curly and Laurey in one fell swoop!"

Gina smiled tentatively. It had never occurred to her that she might not only get the lead in this musical, but have to share it with David!

"If you two wouldn't mind reading for the parts now, we can make this official."

He ran off to get a couple of scripts, and as he did, Gina turned an accusing eye on her husband, demanding under her breath, "When did you ever sing?"

He lifted a shoulder in a lazy gesture. "I was in the boys' choir at school. For three years running, I sang the solo in—"

"Never mind," Gina snapped, her excitement about being in the Maryvale Players' musical waning fast. "What about that John Wayne getup you're wearing? Where in heaven's name did you get it?"

"I made a few calls this afternoon to find out what the musical was. Then I visited the local thrift shop for the jeans. The department store had the rest. Looks pretty authentic, don't you think?"

She sniffed, provoked. He did look authentic—powerfully so—but she refused to admit it. Instead she muttered, "You're going to make a complete fool of yourself, David. Curly says words like *ain't*, *s'sposen* and *brung*. You couldn't do it—not even if you were going to be paid money."

"*S'posen* I did it for love?" he chided with a taunting grin. "If I don't miss my guess, Curly and Laurey will have a kiss from time to time." His smile grew sly and meaningful, and a shaft of dismay sped down her spine.

"If you dare try to slide your tongue..." Unfortunately, Fred was back with the scripts and she thought better of finishing her thought. David was smart enough to get the message.

Winded from his dash up the stairs, Fred said, "Okay, let's try the scene where Curly and Laurey are alone in the orchard. You're holding hands, love-struck. At the end, down here." He pointed on the page. "You might as well go into the song, 'People Will Say We're in Love.' How about it?"

"Sounds great," David replied, taking her hand firmly in his.

Gina's smile was false as she assured Fred. "*That* should establish my acting ability if anything does."

Gina noticed that Fred's expression was perplexed as he left the stage.

Ten minutes later, Gina and David had been given the parts of Curly and Laurey. Gina felt only marginally victorious, considering her leading man. They were leaving the stage to lingering applause when she passed Paul, who was trying out for the part of Jud. He squeezed her arm and prompted, "See, there, I knew you'd get it."

Her smile was sickly. "I guess I'm happy about it."

His encouraging smile wavered. "That man of yours can do just about anything, can't he?"

Gina's lips compressed with determination. "He's not my man! And after tomorrow night, he'll wish he'd never followed me out here."

DAVID HUNG UP THE PHONE and called to Gina, who'd locked herself in the bedroom over an hour before. "They're in Maryvale, now. It'll be twenty minutes until they arrive."

"I'll be ready."

"You're not going to embarrass me, are you?" he asked, worry ripe in his voice.

"I told you, David, I'll be wearing a jacket, skirt and hose. How bad could it be?"

He stared at the closed door, his hands resting on his hips. "And how do I explain the tape across the house? Earthquake damage?"

"I don't care how you explain it. It's your problem, not mine. I never intend to explain myself to those educated snobs again."

"What if I just rip it up?"

"You do, and I'll come out there stark-naked."

"Like you did with the deliveryman?"

There was a long pause before she replied firmly, "Don't remind me of that. I didn't know he was out there. The point is, he lives in town. I'll have to run into him from time to time. The Finchkelps—*I could care less!*"

He pursed his lips and looked down at the damnable tape. Exhaling tiredly, he decided he had little choice. "All right. Put on your clothes. I'll leave the tape."

"Fine," she called. "Let me know when they're here."

David puttered nervously in the kitchen, though the salad was made and in the crisper, the salmon steaks were ready to be popped into a simmering skillet of herbs, and the stuffed eggplants were giving off a delicious aroma from the oven. He'd worked hard on this meal, and he hoped everything would go all right. Quentin would be retiring in two years, and David knew he was high on the list of candidates to replace him as AEI's president. It would be a highly prestigious position, even in Boston, a metropolis filled with prestigious institutes of higher learning.

He checked the warming plate where the spiced-apple dessert simmered. He'd been hard-pressed to put together a menu that didn't conflict with Estelle's dietary demands, but he thought he'd done a good job. Now, if only Gina would cooperate—

There was a hearty knock at the door, and David tensed. The moment was at hand that could make or break his chances of becoming AEI's president.

"Gina," he called as he went to the door. "The Finch-kelps are here."

Pulling the front door wide, he smiled at the squat, bald man and his thin, pinched-faced wife. "Why, hello, Estelle, Quentin. I gather you had no trouble at the bridge."

Quentin, perpetually florid, marched inside, booming delightedly, "Baron, old sport, let me have a look at you. Estelle, doesn't he look fine? Trim and brown as a boot."

David smiled but didn't particularly feel like it. His mind was on the bedroom door that had just clicked open.

Estelle followed her husband inside and repeated meekly, "Fine. David, you look fine."

Ignoring Estelle, Quentin slapped David on the back and said, "Mind if I smoke, old sport? Estelle's allergy to smoke keeps me from doing it in the car, you know."

"If she's allergic to smoke, Quentie, maybe you'd better quit—if not for your own sake, for hers," Gina commented as she came out of the bedroom. Her bizarre appearance stopped David and both his guests dead in their tracks.

She smiled at the three stone-stiff statues, openly gaping at her, and she felt a thrill of triumph. She hadn't lied to David. She was wearing a jacket, skirt and hose—only the jacket was oversize, sequined denim, and the skirt, a wildly printed yellow scarf with a long fringe. She'd tied it at her waist. Clingy and transparent, it covered only a portion of her thighs. Her hose were bright fuchsia and her shoes were studded riding boots. She had on a tie-dyed T-shirt, torn away at her midriff. Across her breasts was emblazoned the command, Don't Think—*Be!*

From one ear dangled a man's antique pocket watch, framed by hair that stood away from her head in all directions, as though it had been blown-dry in a wind tunnel. Lastly, and most disturbingly, her smiling lips were—black.

Estelle made a strangled sound in her throat, and Quentin didn't even try to hide his gasp.

Slowly, reluctantly, David's eyes trailed over his wife and his heart sank. She hated him. She couldn't have shown it more clearly, had she walked directly to him and spat in his face. He closed his eyes, erasing the vision, wishing he could as easily erase the reality.

Gina, noting David's shock, felt a sudden surge of remorse for what she was doing. She really didn't want to humiliate him so much as shake a little stuffing out of the Finchkelps' starched shirts. But by his pained expression, she could see that she was hurting David badly with her shabby game. Forcing herself to keep smiling, she went on with her entrance, but she decided she'd try to repair the damage if she could. Brightly, she exclaimed, "What? No costumes? David didn't you remember to tell Quentin and Estelle this was a 'Come as Your Favorite Singer' dinner?"

He stared blankly at her as she forged on, thinking fast. "It's the latest rage in California, Estelle. You see, I'm, er, Stinking Mama and David's, uh, Julio Iglesias!" She'd pulled the name out of the air, not at all confident that Julio Iglesias ever wore button-down shirts and suspenders.

"Julio Iglesias?" Estelle asked, her expression even more pinched as she turned to look at David.

"Yes. He's a Latin singer who—"

"I know who he is," she interrupted quietly, walking toward David. Peering closely at him, she breathed, "My goodness." Then she suddenly smiled, "I love Julio. You look just like him, except . . ." Shyly, she reached up and tugged a lock of hair down across his forehead. "There. That's better."

"Are you a fan of his?" Gina asked, surprised.

"I simply love him," Estelle murmured. "Quentin, why didn't you tell me this was a costume party? I don't look like anybody."

Gina felt pity for the poor woman who lived her life as The President's Wife. Apparently she was starved for some fun. With a supportive smile, she offered, "You look a little like Doris Day, Estelle. Do you like her? Maybe if we pulled your hair back in a French roll and gave you a few freckles with my eyeliner pencil . . ."

Estelle's face lit and she began to fumble with her fine, shoulder-length gray hair. Pulling it back, she declared. "I think that would help. What else?"

"Well, you see—" Gina was throwing out things now as they flashed through her mind. "We have to call each other by our singer's name and we have to sing when we speak— in their style. Like Doris sings sweet and perky. Understand?"

Estelle was beaming with delight. Obviously she was game for new things. It was too bad not many new things came up in her life.

Quentin was scowling and Gina had a sinking feeling that this ploy wasn't going to fool the correct, hidebound man. He looked from Gina to David and then back to Gina. "I've never heard of such a thing," he groused. Peering pointedly at David, he said, "Old sport, you never even mentioned the party theme to me. And here I could have worn my new Bermuda shorts and come as Don Ho. I've loved Don Ho ever since we made that trip to Hawaii in '76. Remember that, Estelle?"

She was removing her suit jacket and unbuttoning the top two buttons of her high-necked blouse. "Call me Doris, Don." She smiled timidly at him. "And I may let you—be perky with me later."

Gina almost fainted. Gathering her wits, she managed, "Just roll up your pants, Quent. And I can make you a lei from pages of this *Newsweek* and some string. What do you say?"

The older man rubbed his big paws together in anticipation, quick to do as she suggested. After rolling up his pants to expose pasty, bow-legs, he began to gyrate his mammoth hips, singing something about a grass shack in a gritty monotone.

Estelle imitated him, stiffly at first, then, with a giggle, and parroting Doris Day's voice, she warbled along.

David, still nonplused by his guests' transformation, turned to eye Gina doubtfully. "Somehow, I don't think this is what you had in mind. Was it—Stinking Mama?" he queried under his breath.

Gina looked completely shamefaced. "Not in a thousand years."

While Doris and Don broke into a fun-loving argument about whether Don Ho ever really sang "Little Grass Shack," David admonished quietly, "I suppose it was your plan to ruin me."

Gina cast him a sad glance and shook her head. "I don't want to ruin you, David. Just—" She faltered, but made herself say it. "Just don't ruin me."

9

QUENTIN AND ESTELLE were gone. It was midnight and all was quiet. Catching sight of the tape that divided the living-room floor, Gina smiled inwardly. Her explanation that the tape had been laid down for a party game called "Tightrope Walk Across Niagara" had gone over very well. However, when Estelle had won, managing to make it from the lighthouse-tower door all the way to the kitchen table without losing her balance, Gina had been obliged to give up one of her abalone shells as a prize.

Oh, well. The important thing was that the Finchkelps hadn't guessed the truth. Gina realized she'd been foolish to think her plan to embarrass David wouldn't also hurt his career. At least, handling the whole mess the way she had had salvaged his position.

She sank down onto the couch and removed the pocket-watch earring from her ear. Her tired sigh was audible, and David, who had just seated himself in his chair, glanced over at her, remarking, "That thing must have hurt."

Rubbing her lobe, she confessed, "I may die." She chuckled at the absurdity of using her grandfather's pocket watch as an earring. Sitting back and stretching, she said, "You know, I don't think I've ever heard Estelle Finchkelp laugh before this evening. They both seemed to have fun, don't you think?"

His features darkened. "Being courteous people, they know how to accommodate a host and hostess." Indicating her attire with a meaningful nod, he continued, "Even the lunatic fringe."

Gina's chin tilted with affront. "Admit it, David. They even surprised themselves by how much they enjoyed the evening. Maybe too many people with Ph.D.s think they have to behave in a certain way, so they repress their spontaneous side. If that's true, then I pity your stuffy, repressed cronies at AEI."

"Gina," David began softly. "If you want my opinion, you're the one who learned something about yourself tonight."

"Me?" She eyed him doubtfully. "Like what?"

"That you couldn't carry off that farce of yours. You couldn't bring yourself to admit that looking like a victim of toxic groundwater was supposed to be the new you."

She stiffened with resentment. "I didn't do it because I got cold feet," she blurted, feeling hurt. "I did it for you. As long as you insist on connecting yourself to me—well, I thought—oh, I don't know why I bothered!" Throwing up her hands in exasperation, she sputtered, "I—I should have gone ahead with my original plan. You might not have a job now, but you would have gotten the message and left me alone!"

In three strides he was standing before her, pulling her up to sway unsteadily before him. With his fingers securely grasping hers, he accused softly, "You couldn't have done that, Gina. Not to me. We're meant to be together." Pulling her to him, he whispered near her ear, "You care about what happens to me. I thought, for a terrible moment tonight, I'd lost you, but when you made up that crazy party theme, I knew—"

She struggled, not wanting to be affected by his encompassing warmth, his big, expressive hands, his teasing lips as they nipped along her jaw. He was reading this in his own way, as usual! She pressed against his chest, crying breathlessly, "No, David. Don't allow your ego to twist this in your mind to something it wasn't. I told you why I did it and it had nothing to do with anything but—but compassion for you. I know how important the presidency of AEI is—"

His kiss was sudden, urgent, halting her words. He wasn't going to listen to her insistence that it was over between them. David was strong-willed, intent on getting his way.

When he lifted his lips a hairbreadth above her mouth, Gina heard herself sigh. Fearing she was losing control, she cried, "David, you're being unfair—"

"All's fair in love and war, darling," he murmured against her mouth as he lowered them both to the couch. She closed her eyes and allowed her hands to wander on their own to the intimate enticement of his body. It surprised her to discover that she had unbuttoned his shirt and was running her tongue along his jaw. It also surprised her to discover that David had rid her not only of her jacket, but her T-shirt. All that stood in the way of flesh-to-flesh contact was a bit of feminine lace.

She couldn't believe what she was allowing him to do. Her original plan had been to anger him, frustrate him, prove to him that he was nothing to her. But now, she was writhing delightedly beneath him, her fingers quivering at the waistband of his slacks. Her hunger rising, she was on the brink of being swept away by her husband's sexual sorcery.

Something not quite nameable invaded Gina's pleasure-clouded mind and nagged at her. What was it? At first it sounded like a baby's cry, but that was impossible. Then, it finally began to dawn on her that what she was hearing was the frightened wail of a cat. *A cat?*

"Lumper!" She struggled to sit up, then cautioned for quiet with a finger at her lips.

David reluctantly sat up, dragging a hand through his hair. He looked over at her, his eyes narrowed, his expression a mixture of confusion and yearning. "What—"

It came again. Louder. More distressed.

Gina jumped to her feet, ignoring the fact that she was naked above the waist. "Lumper's hurt. Can you hear that?"

He reluctantly stood, looking around. Noticing that the door leading to the lighthouse tower was ajar, he nodded in that direction. "How did that get opened?"

Gina followed his gaze. "Must have happened when you and Quentin went outside so that he could have a smoke. I showed Estelle the files on my lighthouse book that I keep in that old chest of drawers out there."

The cat's dreadful yowl came again.

"Lump's out there," Gina murmured tightly as she rushed toward the door.

David was quick to follow, but when she reached the door, he thrust her her denim jacket. "It's cold out there," he reminded gruffly, not wholly recovered from their encounter on the couch.

She accepted the jacket with a mumbled thank-you, embarrassed at how close she'd come to making a spineless idiot of herself again. Dragging it on, she slipped into the darkened tower. David began to button his shirt against the cold as he groped for the light switch.

Since the tower was never used, and in a state of disrepair, the lights that were located at each landing hadn't been maintained. When the electricity was switched on, only two of the four bulbs worked. Still, it was enough light for Gina to see that Lumper's curiosity had gotten him into trouble.

Some seven feet above the first landing, ten feet above their heads, Lumper was hunched precariously on the end of a section of railing above a gaping space where a portion of stairs had broken away. Apparently the cat had jumped across the space, then bounded up to the rickety railing; but now was too frightened to try to make it back down.

"Oh, goodness!" Gina gasped. "He's so scared."

"I thought cats had good balance. He could get down if he wanted to badly enough."

"He's only got half a tail. Maybe that affects his balance. Besides, cats can't climb down as easily as they climb up. Haven't you ever heard of firemen getting cats out of trees?"

David peered up at the thin tom and groused, "Lump, this is such a cliché. You should be ashamed."

Gina tugged on his shirt. "Don't kid, David. What do we do?"

He turned to eye her skeptically. "I suppose by 'we' you mean me?"

She frowned and looked up at Lumper. "We need to hurry, whatever we do. He might fall."

"So might *we*." David muttered. But without further comment, he headed cautiously up the stairs. They creaked ominously as he began to ascend the first grade.

"Should I come, too?" Gina called.

"It won't hold—" A step broke beneath David's weight, and he had to catch himself to keep from falling through. Between clenched teeth, he finished, "Both of us."

"I—I believe you." Her voice was a frail whisper.

Lumper made another pitiful noise, but this time he seemed to know help was on the way.

"I'm coming, I'm coming," David mumbled. The steps wailed in protest and there was a shudder in the whole structure. Grabbing at the railing, David held on.

Gina stifled a scream, and stared unblinking, feeling helpless.

When the scaffolding of aged wood stabilized, David continued on with agonizing slowness. As soon as he reached the first landing, he found that he could only stretch high enough to get Lumper if he rested one foot on the brick wall. To do that, he had to lean precariously over the landing's edge. As he spread-eagled himself across the gaping space almost twenty feet above the cement floor, Gina swallowed hard, clutching her hands together so tightly her nails dug into her skin.

When he was as steady as the awkward position would allow, he snatched at the upper railing. The rough wood wobbled as he touched it, frightening Lumper so badly that he made a mad leap.

"*Ouch!* Damn it, cat, leave some skin!" David growled, as Lumper used his claws to catch himself on his rescuer's shoulders.

Gina's hands were so sweaty she rubbed them on her jacket. Biting her lip, she tried not to distract David with horror-stricken screams.

With Lumper hanging on for dear life, David pushed off the railing and the wall at the same time to give himself enough propulsion to sway back to the relative safety of the landing.

As he let go of the railing, a long section gave way and went crashing to the floor. Gina watched with dread, her heart going to her throat. The light was so dim, she couldn't be positive it was nothing more than a six-foot length of two-by-fours. It seemed an eternity before David and his cowering fur collar reached the cement floor.

When David was finally standing before her, she knew there was more than a little truth to what he'd said before. She did love the man. It was a tragedy that, for the sake of her mental health, she couldn't live the rest of her life with him.

Wearing Lumper like a fur piece, he took a calming breath and leaned heavily against the cold brick wall. "Well, Lump, I believe this is your floor." Lifting the animal from his shoulders he handed him to Gina. "Let's keep the damn door closed from now on. Okay?"

She cuddled the frightened cat in her arms and nodded. Shaking with reaction, she whispered, "David, you could have been killed. I know you're not crazy about heights." Near tears, she focused her eyes on his somber expression. "Thank you. I had no idea you had it in you."

His narrowed gaze searched her face. "What?"

"Heroism, I guess."

He grunted. "If heroism is the same as foolishness, then I'm sure I do."

She touched his arm. "It was foolish to risk your life that way, I suppose, but it was gallant." Feeling an unwanted softness for him, she kissed his jaw. "It's nice to know you can at least care about the needs of a helpless animal."

Turning away, she left him standing there, upset from the dangerous climb, his back stinging from the scratches left by Lumper's panicked clutches. When the door closed between them, he could only stare in disbelief.

"Are you trying to say I don't care about your needs?" he muttered, angry. When he'd had a few minutes to digest her words, he grew less angry with her and more cross with himself. Maybe it wouldn't kill him to admit there were things she'd been doing lately that he could live with. Certainly not the crazy clothes or the death-defying diet, but there were—things. He couldn't fault her strength. He admired it. And she was compassionate. Against his will, he admitted, even in his frustration and anger with her tonight, there had been moments when he'd actually been amused by her oddball sense of play. He'd never seen the Finchkelps so lighthearted. If anything, her plan had backfired, and she'd made him look even better in their eyes.

He supposed he should have admitted that to her, but his irritation over her attempted sabotage had hurt, overshadowing everything else.

THE NEXT AFTERNOON, Gina decided to go down to the beach to study her lines. She'd worked all morning on her book and thought the first three chapters were shaping up nicely. Despite David's interference, she felt she was managing to get into a fairly productive routine.

The breeze was pleasant and cool, ruffling her hair and the pages of her script. She couldn't have been in a better mood. Smiling, she lifted her hair off her shoulders and closed her eyes, attempting to commit Laurey's first speech to memory.

"Want to run some lines with me?" David asked, startling Gina. She twisted around on her beach towel to squint up at him. His body was silhouetted by the bright sun, enveloping him in a luminous radiance. The effect was breathtaking.

"Been jogging, I see," she commented, exhibiting what she hoped was aloof disinterest, though his closeness had a breath-quickening effect on her.

"A while ago." He squatted near her towel. "What do you say? Would you like to go over a scene with me?"

She flipped a page. "I need to memorize my speech—"

"Gina?" he broke in, his voice sounding very close. "Do you know what day this is?"

She blinked up from her script, alert, but didn't turn to face him. "Yes. It's my thirtieth birthday. Why?"

"Happy Birthday," he whispered near her ear. Suddenly, one pink rose appeared before her as he added, "There are eleven more up at the house."

She stared at the long-stemmed blossom, chewing on her lower lip. After a brief hesitation, she took it and lifted it to her nose, inhaling its heavy sweetness. Cautiously, she turned to face him. His expression was solemn, and in his eyes she could see the shadow of sadness. Her stupid heart did a flip-flop and she smiled faintly. "It's lovely. But you really shouldn't have."

"Don't say that. I wanted to." He smiled back, but his eyes remained somber. "I'll let you get back to work." Rising, he turned to walk away.

Gina frowned, noticing the ugly scratches that spoiled the flawlessness of his back, and called out his name.

He halted and half turned.

"Your back!" she exclaimed. "Did Lumper do that?"

He shrugged, his grin askew.

Her irritation vanished, and she was startled to find that she was on her feet, walking toward him. Gingerly she touched one of the scratches, and felt more than saw him tense. "Did you put anything on these?"

"Soap and water."

"Come on." She took his arm. "I've got some salve."

They were almost to the lighthouse door when she offered, "When we've disinfected those scratches, I'll go over the first scene with you."

He glanced at her, surprised.

She sniffed the rose again. "The flowers were a lovely thought."

"Pink roses suit your skin tone." He smiled fondly. "I could never understand why you preferred yellow roses.

They make your skin look so sallow. That's why I've always guided you away from yellow clothes."

"But yellow is such a happy color," she defended, her obliging mood fading fast. He was doing it again—controlling again. Taking a deep breath, she lifted her eyes to scan his profile, and very quietly asked, "Do you know what I would have liked better than pink roses?"

He was halfway through the door when her words halted him. Turning, he looked down at her. "No. What?"

"Chocolates."

"Chocolates! But they're—"

"I know," she interrupted, sadly, having heard it all before. "They're fattening, high in cholesterol and—" she paused to warily meet his gaze. "And I love them. If you really cared about my wants and needs, you'd have given me a box of chocolates. Pink roses are what *you* wanted me to have, not what *I* wanted."

"That's ridiculous," he countered, but so softly she could barely hear it.

She had an urge to touch his cheek, but resisted it, whispering sadly, "David, don't expect to be thanked when you force things on people that they don't want."

A look of disgust flashed across his face and he muttered grimly, "I give up—"

"Good! Finally!" Flinching from his condemning stare, she hurried on, "I'll let Fred Potter know you're going back to Boston," she retorted, startled by the bleakness in her voice. "There's still time to replace you in the part of Curly."

"Like hell, I'm going back to Boston!" he growled, his eyes glittering with fury.

"But—but you just said—"

"A *damned* figure of speech, Gina. You know, like, 'You drive me crazy'? Right now, though, that's pretty close to the truth!" Turning away, he crossed to the bedroom and slammed the door behind him.

In misery, Gina stared down at the rose in her hand. On leaden feet she walked to the end table beside the couch and placed the blossom in the vase with the others. The arrangement was lovely, accented by greenery and a feathery array of baby's breath. A card was attached to the mauve velvet ribbon. Listlessly she opened it and stared glumly. Inside was the single word "Forever," written in David's bold, precise script.

Forever! she thought brutally, trying to ignore the sudden twist of pain that tore through her. Swiping at a tear, she crumpled the card and let it fall to the floor, murmuring sadly, "Figure of speech...."

DECIDING TO BE STUBBORN, that evening, they took separate cars to the rehearsal. Gina arrived first, and was greeted by Paul, who had lost out to Max Murphy for the part of the villian, Jud Fry. Gina tried to console him by telling Paul he could never play a character so dirty and twisted. "You'll be much better playing the happy-go-lucky Will." She added, "To be honest, I feel sure Max will do great justice to the vulgar Jud character."

Paul's cheeks pinkened. "I know why you're irritated at him," he confided. "He told me about seeing you—er—"

Gina threw up a halting hand, "Don't say it! *Good grief!* How many people has he told?"

"Don't know. Everybody, I suppose."

"Oh, for heaven's sake!" She scowled. "Max is no gentleman."

With a meek smile, he said, "Ol' Max fancies himself a stud."

"I gathered. He's about as subtle as he is gentlemanly," she declared. Looking around, she saw him lounging against the stage, smoking. An obvious bodybuilder, he was clad in a red muscle-shirt and tight jeans. Seeing he'd caught her eye, he winked and waved. Turning back to Paul, she protested, "I'll have no trouble struggling with that conceited lug when he tries to kiss me in the play."

Paul looked chagrined. "I have to admit that's mainly why I wanted the part—to kiss you." He blushed. "Sneaky, huh?"

She shook her head at him. "You've already kissed me. Remember?"

"Yes—I do." The remark sounded wistful.

Gina was uncomfortable. "Well—you might really enjoy playing Iduna's boyfriend."

His eyebrows dipped as he considered that. "I suppose it's better than nothing."

Gina decided it was time to change the subject when Max sidled up, carrying a folding chair. Dropping it beside hers, he joined them. "Hi, Paul, pretty lady," he said, his cigarette dangling from one corner of his mouth. Surveying her up and down with insulting thoroughness, he announced, "Lookin' good."

Gina ground her teeth. She'd had enough of this man's leering and suggestive remarks. Vaulting up, she retorted, "Listen, Max, I've heard you told everybody about seeing me—er—unclothed. I think that was dirty pool, and you were out of line to do it!"

"Hey, sorry. I sure don't want to hack you off." With a contrite smile, he removed the cigarette from his lips and flicked ashes on the floor. "I'll be a good boy. Forgive me?"

She eyed him with irritation, then said, "Promise me you'll never mention that day again, okay?"

He took a long drag and half smiled. "Sure, sure. I'm darned sorry, Gina."

Relenting a little, but knowing she would never completely trust Max, she offered, "Well—all right. After all, we will be working together in this musical."

He grinned and stood, dropping his butt and crushing it beneath his boot heel. "That's true. As Jud, I'm gonna be hot after your bod." He laughed. "Talk about typecasting."

"See! It's remarks like that—"

He planted his hands on her shoulders. "Calm down. I couldn't resist." Winking, he said, "See you later, pretty lady." With a disdainful half-turn he glanced down at Paul. "Makin' your macho move, Romeo?" he teased.

Gina sat back down. Disgusted, she watched Max's retreat, scoffing, "That man just *oozes* charm!"

Paul snorted. "Gets on my nerves."

"Join the club."

"Not that I'm dying to change the subject, but Idi's pretty mad at you," Paul confided. "She wanted to play Laurey awfully badly, especially when David got the part of Curly."

Gina looked over at the beauty-shop owner, sitting silently, studying her lines. She was dressed in snug jeans and a close-fitting knit top. Unexpectedly their eyes met, and Iduna smiled, but there was no friendship in her expression. Gina turned back to look at Paul. "She's not the only one who wishes she had the part. It's going to be a royal pain for me."

Gina didn't see David come in, but she could tell when he did. Iduna and several of the other female cast members glanced up. Idi scrambled to her feet and hurried toward the door. Gina was near enough to hear her say, "Why, David Baron, it's so nice to meet you." The jeans-clad woman ushered him off, and Gina couldn't hear anymore. It didn't really matter, she told herself sternly.

Nevertheless, several times she found her attention drifting away from what Paul was saying to notice Iduna chatting gaily away with David.

"Okay, everybody," Fred shouted. "Let's get this show on the road." He clapped his hands for attention. "First up, I need Laurey and Curly."

The scene with David and Gina went more smoothly than she thought it would. There had been no physical contact, but quite a bit of high temper had been required. Curly expected Laurey to go to the barn dance with him, and Laurey didn't like being taken for granted. *Had that hit home!* Gina had had a ball being belligerent and defiant. She didn't know if it was her acting ability or her need to snipe at David that made the scene go well, but Fred had nothing but compliments for them when it was over.

The dancers were now working out choreography, and Gina was enjoying a soft drink with Paul, but she couldn't help but notice when Iduna grabbed David's hand, drawing him into another conversation.

"What are you looking at?" Paul asked, his tone leery. "You haven't heard a word I've said."

She jerked around to face him. "I have, too. You were talking about—about—the next scene." It had sounded more like a question than a statement.

He shrugged it off. "Never mind. Probably my paranoid imagination."

Gina found herself looking reluctantly around for David. He'd moved, but not far from Iduna. He was lounging against a wall, clad in those infernal tight jeans and a red flannel shirt, talking to her.

"What do you think she's up to?" Gina asked, indicating Idi with a nod.

Paul chuckled wickedly. "What do you think? And the kinkier the better."

Gina stared covertly at Idi and David. The striking brunette began to toy with a button on his shirtfront, and Gina felt a shaft of malice run up her spine.

"What are you thinking, Gina?" Paul prompted. "You've got a terrible frown on your face."

She pulled her gaze away from the cozy couple to glance at him. "Thinking? Me? Nothing at all," she quipped, trying not to dwell on David and his companion. It wasn't her business, after all—or, at least, it soon wouldn't be.

He eyed her doubtfully but didn't express his thoughts. "So, do you want to run over this scene?"

She nodded, not really interested. For some reason, a hard, unhappy knot had formed in her stomach.

"Or would you rather run over Iduna?" he asked, drawing her gaze from the page.

"What did you say?" Gina knew she couldn't have heard him right.

10

"GINA," PAUL PROMPTED quietly, "you either have to give him up or take him back. Being jealous when you profess to want to be rid of him isn't very rational."

Gina's lips dropped open in surprise. "Jealous? Me?" she protested. "And just who am I supposed to be jealous of?"

Paul shrugged. "Iduna, would be my guess. She's the one who's trying to undress your husband."

Gina sniffed scornfully. "I couldn't care less. Let's get to work on that scene."

He eyed her critically for a moment, but she pretended not to notice as she flipped through her script to find the right page. She was having just the tiniest bit of trouble with some nagging resentfulness toward Iduna. Why, she couldn't fathom. After all, she didn't want David. She supposed her discomfort at seeing him flirt with another woman was out of force of habit more than anything else. One just couldn't sever ten years of emotional ties as if they were a piece of twine. She felt sure that once David was back in Boston and out of her house, she would be able to forget him completely.

"Because, you see," Paul went on doggedly, "if you're still in love with him, then maybe I'd better give up on you."

Gina was startled by his directness, and cast him an anxious look. "I'm certainly not still in—" She faltered. "Okay, maybe I still have some feeling for him, but he knows the reason I'm leaving him isn't because I don't care about him. It's because— Well, you know."

Paul sat back in his folding chair and crossed his arms before him, eyeing her silently. When he finally spoke, he asked, "And he refuses to make any compromises to keep you?"

Gina sighed heavily. "David has a commanding personality. His idea of compromise is letting me go and then coming with me! In the final analysis, he gets his way. That's no equal relationship, Paul. That's a dictatorship. Nothing positive can flourish in an atmosphere like that."

"So, you're saying you don't mind Idi's attentions to him?"

She shot David and Iduna a piercing glance. "I wish Iduna luck. But I figure she'll end up running for her life, too, when she finds out she'll lose every shred of her free will in the trade."

Paul made a sound—whether of disbelief or satisfaction, Gina couldn't tell. She turned to face him again. "What was that for?"

He smiled at her with a mixture of affection and worry. "Now, for the big-money question. Is there hope for me?"

She stilled. Why did she suddenly feel desolate and cold? At least for now, there was no hope at all for Paul. Trying to be diplomatic, she touched his hand fondly, murmuring, "Give me some time. After all, I'm not even divorced yet."

They were interrupted when Fred called for the next scene. Gina and David were both in it, so she patted Paul's hand and left him sitting there. "See you later." With a brief smile, she hurried to the front of the auditorium.

Still stark and devoid of scenery, the stage was strewn with a few props to assist in these first, rough rehearsals. There was a sawhorse, a stool and two scarred wooden chairs. Fred was moving things around and calling out, "And this sawhorse will represent the front of the barn. Okay, we'll need to get Curly and Laurey familiar with their dance, but for now, they can walk through it. After that, we'll do the scene where Jud confronts Laurey behind the barn. Got it?"

Gina and David were suddenly face-to-face. His nostrils flared as he took her determinedly in his arms for the dance. He seemed angry. Was he angry with her? After his little "unbutton-my-shirt" episode with Idi, David had some nerve to be angry with her!

"Did you and Paul have fun?" he probed roughly.

She was confused. "Fun? I don't understand. We were running over a few lines."

"Do you hold hands with everyone you run over the lines with?"

She shot him a glacial stare. "Do you allow all second leads to unbutton your shirt?"

His lips twisted sardonically. "Feeling insecure?"

"Insec— Not on your life!" she retorted, her cheeks going hot. "And, I'd appreciate it if you'd keep your conversation limited to the scene we're doing."

"Whatever you say, my love," he taunted, his voice deceptively gentle. "Can you two-step?"

"No. But then, neither can you."

"What makes you think that?"

She grew wary. "Don't tell me you did the solo two-step at London's Harthrow Gentlemen's Academy, too?"

"All right, I won't." The slow twisting of his lips sent a shiver of apprehension up her spine. Maybe he really could two-step. After all, he did spend the first ten years of his life in Texas—two-stepping country. She swallowed, wondering what she was in for.

Marjorie began to play "Territory Folks Should Stick Together," and what was supposed to have been a walk-through, turned into a full-fledged hoedown. Gina was shuffled and pranced backward all over the stage, struggling as well as she could to keep up with the unfamiliar Western dance. Her troubles were compounded since David insisted upon molding his hips and thighs into hers.

When Marjorie's accompaniment came to a stop, Gina was a nervous wreck. David had managed to bump and grin his erotic message into her lower extremities and, frustrating her beyond good sense, had made her feel weak all over. How she hated his ability to know a woman's sensual breaking point and exactly how to achieve it!

She forced her memorized line from between clenched jaws. "Get away with you, Curly. I saw you eyein' Gertie!" Her nerve endings sizzling from his carnal sabotage, she shoved harder than necessary to remove herself from his embrace. A milking stool happened to be directly behind David, and Gina's push made him stumble backward into it, and he toppled. In what seemed like slow motion, he plunged off the front of the stage.

Gina saw him disappear below the footlights and gasped. Hurrying to the side, she dropped to her knees and cried, "Oh, my Lord, I've killed him!"

He landed on his back and lay ominously still. A frightening few seconds passed before he shook his head and came slowly up on one elbow.

"David, you're alive!" Gina cried, clambering down to take him in her arms. "Is anything broken? How are you feeling?"

He lifted his pained gaze to her and queried sarcastically, "Was it good for you?" It came out in a half groan.

Gina frowned, fearing he'd addled his brains. "I—I don't understand."

His gaze—severe—raked her stricken face. "Dammit, Gina, I've put up with a lot from you, lately. Will you never stop and think before you act?"

"But David," Gina countered weakly, shocked by his outburst, "you must realize this was an accident."

"Like hell," he growled. "You keep playing your games, and you're going to get someone killed."

Several of the cast members who'd gathered around began to murmur uncomfortably as David shrugged to a sitting position.

"Don't you talk to her that way, Baron," Max interjected acidly, barreling to the front of the crowd.

David squinted up at the redheaded man but said nothing.

"David, please," Gina pleaded. "I didn't deliberately—"

Raising a hand to his head, he retorted, "Tell it to somebody who gives a damn."

Fred had come over and knelt beside David to examine his injury. "Doesn't look too bad, Curly. Calm down. You'll be okay."

Several of the other cast members moved to help him to his feet, all suggesting he needed to relax, and that everything was going to be all right.

When David was standing, flanked by several concerned people, he shifted his broad shoulder so that he could glare down at Gina. "I'd appreciate it if you could restrain yourself in future from these juvenile dramatics." Fury darkening his tone, he chided, "*Try* to grow up."

Gina was so stunned, she could only sit mutely, unable to defend herself.

Iduna appeared suddenly, carrying a plastic bag of ice. "Don't excite yourself David. I've had Red Cross training." Taking his arms, she assisted him to a bench near the wall. Settling beside him, she placed the cold pack on the back of his head and situated herself so that he could rest against her shoulder. "Anything you need, you just let me know."

Though her legs felt weak from fright over David's public scolding, Gina began to struggle to her feet.

Paul came to her rescue, helping her to stand. "You're pretty shaken," he said. "Let's get out of here. Fred would understand. You need to get away for a while."

She shook her head. "No, thanks, Paul." Though the idea of escaping and comforting herself with Paul's supportive company and a hot-fudge sundae seemed inviting, she knew she couldn't do it. She wouldn't run out on her responsibilities here, or the rest of the cast, no matter how hard David had made the job of staying. "Excuse me—Paul. I should apologize," she murmured, her words shaky.

"I ought to punch him out," snarled Max.

Gina shook her head at the man. "Leave it alone—everybody."

"You, too, Gina. You have nothing to apologize for," Paul protested weakly, but she was already moving away from him.

On quivering legs, she forced herself to walk over to where David was sitting. Meeting his indignant stare bravely, she offered, "I know you're in pain, David, and I'm sure when you feel better, you'll realize I would never wish injury on you. Still, I'm sorry for causing your fall." She turned her back, and with as much dignity as she could muster, marched stiffly away from him.

David focused a brooding gaze at her retreating form. His head throbbing unmercifully, he grimaced at the realization that he'd made a first-class ass out of himself and completely underestimated his wife. Looking around, he saw that more than a few people were staring openly at him, horrified at his nasty treatment of Gina. He groaned, furious with himself. Taking it wrong, Iduna began to fuss with the ice pack. She couldn't know that his distress had been because he'd acted like a bastard, rather than anything as trivial as a near concussion.

Just who was the childish one this time, Baron? he berated himself harshly. As Iduna cooed and simpered near his ear, David made a silent promise. Gina would get an apology at the first possible opportunity—as soon as he could stand up without feeling dizzy.

Gina didn't stop walking until she'd gone up onto the stage and retreated behind the curtain. She wanted to hide. No, she wanted to die. How could David have done that to her? How could he have treated her like a naughty child? Feeling shamed, she hugged herself, stifling a mortified shiver. Could she ever face these people again?

There was a tap on her shoulder. Startled, Gina twisted around to see Fred Potter standing there, a regretful smile lifting his lips. "It'll be okay, Laurey," Fred assured her. "People lose their tempers and say things they don't mean. Just forget it." With a comforting squeeze of her arm, he added, "I think getting back to work would help get everybody's mind off it. Why don't we do that scene with you and Jud, if you wouldn't mind."

"Okay, Fred," she agreed with as much enthusiasm as one might if she were about to have her teeth extracted with a pair of rusty pliers.

Fred winked encouragingly and patted her arm. "You're a trouper, kid."

As he called for the scene, Gina walked onstage, her shoulders squared, her heart hammering. With one disheartened glance at David and his doting Florence Nightingale, she moved to meet Max at center stage, determined to push them both out of her mind.

Max and Gina went through their scene. It didn't go very well. Gina's depression over David's rudeness haunted her, not to mention the fact that she had to struggle with Max as he forced a kiss on her. He certainly put everything into the part. All in all, it wasn't her happiest experience to date.

Twenty minutes later, they'd finally made it all the way through the scene. For some reason Max kept flubbing his lines just at the part where he had to kiss her—over and over. Gina was about to cry foul when Fred finally announced, "Okay, folks, it's nearly ten o'clock. I figure I'll have Jud and Laurey go through this once more and then we'll call it quits. The rest of you are free to go."

Gina's stomach constricted, but recalling that Fred had called her a trouper, she decided to keep her complaints to herself. Instead, she consulted her script, trying to concentrate on her lines and hoping Max was doing the same. It took her a minute to realize someone was calling her name. Turning toward the front of the stage, she saw David standing at the place where he'd fallen. His hands were curled over the ledge that held the footlights; his expression was solemn.

Apprehensively, she asked, "Yes? Did you say something to me?"

"I'm very sorry, Gina," he began, his voice soft and contrite. "I was a bastard, before."

Max laughed harshly, "That's about the size of it, Baron. What you need is a swift kick in the butt."

A brief, sad smile twisted David's lips, but he didn't take his eyes from Gina, remarking quietly, "I hope that's not the only way I can be prodded into moving forward." His gaze haunted, he asked, "Can you forgive me?"

Even blighted and watchful as his expression was, David's face was captivating, and she felt a blow to her heart. "David, I—"

"Sure, she'll forgive you," Max cut in sharply. "Just as soon as you aim your tail back toward Boston and leave her alone!"

David shifted to stab Max with a cutting glare. "I could engage you in a battle of wits, Murphy," he assured in a controlled voice. "But I don't relish firing on the walking wounded."

"Is that a crack?" Max protested.

David half smiled. "Yours, I might add, is obviously a head wound."

"Why, you—"

"Max . . ." Gina took hold of his sleeve as he began to advance on David. "Stay out of this." Turning toward David, she managed a strained smile. "I accept your apology. Now maybe you'd better go."

David nodded, and Gina was touched by the gentle sadness in his eyes. "Thank you. And I—"

"Yeah, yeah, yeah. We've got a rehearsal here, Baron. Remember?" Max interrupted hotly.

David chose not to acknowledge the other man's hostility. Pursing his lips, he nodded a farewell to Gina and turned away.

THE FIRST WEEK OF rehearsals was behind them and the scenery was well on the way to completion. To Gina's relief, David had been much less critical all week. But he'd still dominated her every waking hour by his obstinate presence, both at the lighthouse and at rehearsals.

He was intentionally making things difficult for her at rehearsals. They seemed always to be required to dance together, hold hands or, worst of all, to *kiss*, and David used each opportunity to his single-minded advantage.

Gina had managed to maneuver things, make excuses, whatever she could invent to keep from having to kiss him during rehearsals—up to now. But, tonight, they were going to rehearse the grand finale, and she didn't think she could call a halt just before the kiss by pleading a headache, a splinter in her finger, or to ask questions about her character's motivation. She'd used up her delaying tactics, and she was as nervous as a mouse in a cage with a starving cat. There was an unmistakable, predatory glitter in David's eyes. It told her that she was going to be kissed tonight, and she was going to be kissed damn thoroughly.

Their eyes had happened to meet moments before, and David had passed her such a vile grin she's almost fallen out of her chair. She fiddled with a loose string dangling from a rip in her hacked-up jeans and secretly surveyed him as he chatted with several smitten females.

For several nights following rehearsals, David had come in quite late. Still when Paul asked Gina out, and she had begged off with a variety of excuses out of a demented curiosity to see whether David went home or not. Most evenings, he hadn't, but her pride had not allowed her to question him. Still, she couldn't help but wonder where he was spending so much time.

Fred, needing to instruct the stagehands about a quick scenery change, called for a ten-minute break before the finale. Gina escaped to a small room backstage that housed the pop machine. She was flipping the tab on a diet soda when David appeared beside her.

"Diet?" he queried.

She regarded him with indignant eyes, not caring to admit that she'd had a dreadful time getting her jeans fastened this morning. Instead, she informed him stiffly, "They're out of Chocolate Fudge Splash."

"What a shame." His lips twitched knowingly. "Are you about ready for—our scene?"

"Shouldn't I be?" she replied, straining to be distantly polite.

"I thought you might be feeling some reluctance," he taunted.

"You couldn't be more wrong," she retorted, but there was a breathless, agitated quality in her voice that disclosed her dread.

"That's good." He lifted her can of soda pop from her hand and took a drink of it. When he handed the soda back, Gina took a drink herself. She had the feeling David found some pleasure in knowing that her lips were touching something his lips had recently brushed. Her cheeks grew warm at the thoughts and she shifted uncomfortably. Trying to be nonchalant, she reproached, "You're not going to try anything funny, are you?"

He eyed her skeptically. "Funny?" Lounging back against the pop machine, he folded his arms. If it hadn't been for the flash of aggravation in his eyes, she might have believed he was completely at ease. "I assure you, darling, I'm completely serious about—this."

The small room suddenly seemed uncomfortably warm. Casting her gaze down, she feigned interest in the tab in her soda-pop can. "Don't humiliate me, David," she pleaded wearily.

After a long, tense pause, Gina heard him shift away from the pop machine. "I'll see you onstage," he ground out. An instant later, the rap of his boots against the wooden floor told her that he was stalking away.

Fred called for the finale to begin, and Gina took one last gulp of her soda before she tossed it in the trash and headed into the auditorium, toward what she was sure would be an unhappy fate. David would definitely punish her now. Jamming her hands into her jeans pockets, she trudged toward the stage like a convict going to the gallows. She doubted very seriously that her punishment would be boring—not for her, and not for anyone who had the dubious privilege of witnessing it.

THE FINALE WAS progressing at warp speed as far as Gina was concerned. Curly had been acquitted of killing Jud, who'd fallen on his own knife. Flirtatious Ado Annie had been tamed by her stocky swain, Will. And the cast was belting out the final reprise of "Oh, What a Beautiful Mornin'." Curly—gorgeous and virile—leaned against a cardboard tree, one booted heel hiked against it, a trim hip cocked to one side in a sexy slouch. He was smiling at her, his eyes gleaming with desire. And rightly so. Curly and Laurey were about to leave for their honeymoon.

As established by the director, during the final verse of the song, Curly was supposed to amble over to where Laurey was perched on the porch railing, lift her slowly down, and as she descended, she was to kiss his upturned face. Then, he was to do one full turn with Laurey held high in his arms before lowering her to her feet. All the while they were to continue to kiss—even as the music faded and the curtain fell.

Gina was not thrilled about this bit of direction, but she didn't seem to have much choice. The final verse was upon them and Curly was ambling toward her. His eyes twinkled with contrary mirth. But what could he do here in front of thirty-odd cast members and stagehands?

She held fast to her character's "shy bride" smile as he put his hands about her waist and lifted her from the porch rail. The song swelled and the Maryvale players put every ounce of their singing talent into the final, romantic stanzas. Gina hesitantly placed her arms about his neck and, as the script dictated, lowered her lips to his. She, however, didn't give a hoot about the script's dictates on the actual kiss, and kept her mouth defiantly closed.

David didn't seem particularly daunted by this, and as he made his unhurried turn, he nipped tenderly at her lower lip. Between soft bites, he teased her mouth with his dastardly tongue. Irritated by his appalling lack of discretion, Gina hissed, "Don't—"

The fleeting lapse in her defense was enough. Her lips parted, and David chuckled, his charged kiss taking immediate command. His tongue breached her mouth and began to play an unfair game. As her mind whirled with shock and surprise at this sudden, sensory onslaught, she was vaguely aware that she was being lowered slowly toward the floor, and almost as quickly, she realized that something was very wrong—something besides the fact that David had gotten his way, after all. Her left leg wasn't coming down with her.

She mumbled a groan of discomfort against David's devouring mouth. Apparently he was also aware of something amiss, for he lifted his face from hers. "What the hell . . ." he muttered, his gaze darting down.

They both stared. Gina was still being held fast by David, but one of the large slashes in her jeans, high on her left thigh, had managed to gobble up his silver belt buckle like a button in a buttonhole.

Gina was holding on to his neck in an effort to keep her pants from being irreparably torn. "Carry me to the steps. We can unhook over there."

Members of the chorus began to quit singing a few at a time, until the whole finale faded in a confusion of voices.

Some of the more observant singers began to point and chuckle.

When David had settled Gina on a step, allowing her to stand on one leg, he began to struggle with the ensnared belt buckle. Unfortunately the jeans were fairly shredded in that area, and getting all the thin strands out of the way took dexterity and two hands, which neither of them had to spare.

"Don't tear my pants, David," Gina cautioned.

"Why? Would the fashion police arrest you for an unauthorized rip?" he chided. "Hold still."

"You're very droll. Next year you ought to try out for the Physics Follies. Call yourself The Hilarious Mr. Inert Gases—or something simple, like Redshift Skelton."

"I see you've picked up some physics jargon over the years," David observed easily. "Lord, your jeans are tight. How do you breathe?"

"Mind your own business."

"This is what a diet of chocolate and fried chicken does."

"Don't lecture me," Gina hissed. "I'll eat what I please."

"Do you know what your basic problem is, Gina?"

"No, but I'm sure you're going to tell me."

"You need to get laid," he accused softly.

"You need a cold shower," she observed tartly, but felt a blush warm her face.

He merely chuckled, provoking her further. But she decided to concentrate on separating herself from him rather than having a heated argument at such close quarters. In order to get into the right position to dislodge his buckle and keep from ripping the denim any further, David had to press them, groin to groin. "Can you hold the fabric open with one hand?"

"Yes! Just hurry!" She did the best she could, since she had to hold on to his neck to keep from toppling backward and tearing her jeans all the way to her waist. "I've got it opened," she said. "Now thrust up while I arch back."

He lifted his amused gaze to meet her frown and teased, "Oh, baby, I love it when you tell me what you want."

She must have been on the brink of hysteria. That was the only reason she could think of that would have prompted her to burst out laughing. But there was something about this whole ridiculous situation, coupled with David's incorrigible banter, that sent her into a giggling fit. "You're making me crazy. Just do it, for Pete's sake!" she pleaded.

With one more thrust that Gina could have sworn was more blatantly sexual than necessary, she found herself disengaged from her unruly husband. She would have staggered backward and fallen if he hadn't still had an arm about her waist. Reflexively she grabbed his neck, and they were suddenly, once again, clasped cheek to cheek.

The cast was laughing, enjoying the spectacle. Unable to help herself, Gina grinned, thoroughly embarrassed. "That was humiliating," she admitted near his ear.

"One of the pitfalls of being on fashion's cutting edge, I would imagine."

She leaned back, eyeing him narrowly, then shook her head. She was about to make a remark about his contrary wit when Fred said, "Okay, people, we'd better try that again. I want to see this thing through to the finish at least once tonight."

Gina sobered instantly. Try it again! She shot an alarmed look at David, who had the audacity to wink at her.

"Don't you dare try that tongue thing again," she warned.

"Sweetheart, you know me better than that," he countered, his grin perfectly indecent. Before she could protest further, he lifted her in his arms and deposited her on the porch railing.

She grabbed at the wooden prop to keep from falling backward. By the time she'd balanced herself and looked up to glare at David, he had swung around and was meandering away with a grace that bordered on insolence, his broad shoulders straining at the denim jacket he was wearing. *The self-satisfied, obstinate, pacifist—bully!* she mused belligerently.

Clamping her jaw shut, she vowed that this time she would be more prudent. This time she would make no fatal protests. David could nip and lick at the sealed bulwark of her lips until hell became a seaside resort, but she would *not* open her mouth!

11

DAVID TOWERED ABOVE the others, tall and athletic looking in his snug jeans and chambray shirt as he ambled out
of the library after the rehearsal was over. His hat brim
was pulled low over a self-satisfied countenance as he
strode toward Gina. With a finger to the brim of his hat,
he said, "Well—good night, Gina."

Startled by his unexpected departure, she veered around
to stare after him, but he was already disappearing into the
unlit parking lot. "Where—" she began, but broke off her
question. She mustn't allow David to think she cared
about his unexplained absences after rehearsals.

He was just manipulating her again—giving her something to worry about. He thought she'd wonder where he
was spending his time. He might even think she would
torment herself about where he was and who he might be
with. Silly him. "You can go anywhere you want, indulge
in anything you want with anyone you choose, Dr. Baron!
See if I care!" she muttered irritably, heading toward her
car.

"Say, Gina," a voice called from behind her. Recognizing Fred's husky shout, she turned around to look for him
in the crowd. "Some of us are going to the drugstore for a
cup of coffee. Want to come?"

She didn't particularly relish being alone with her
thoughts, so she called, "I'd love to go, Fred. Thanks."

She had no idea who was going to the drugstore, and she
didn't care. She just wanted to be surrounded by happy,

trivial chatter for a change. A half-dozen cast members headed toward the drugstore. It was closed, but since the owner's wife, Erma, was playing the part of Auntie Eller, she opened up the soda fountain. Those cast members who'd come to the drugstore decided to make a party of it and pitched in to create bizarre sundaes and banana splits.

"Gluttons of the world, unite!" cried Erma's husband, Hawley. He raised a spoonful of strawberry ice cream coated with butterscotch syrup and downed it.

"Yeah, let's go for the gusto!" Fred declared, laughing. "Speaking of gusto, I need more whipped cream, Erma. And sugar sprinkles. How about you, Laurey?"

Gina sat back, feeling like an overblown balloon. Her jeans felt like they were about to split at the seams. With a tired shake of her head, she sighed, "Can't eat another sprinkle. You could rent me out right now as the Goodyear blimp." Pushing herself up from her place at the end of the booth, she said, "I'd better go. The walk back to the parking lot will do me good."

"You want company?" Fred asked. "Although I doubt if anything bad would happen to you here in Maryvale."

She patted his shoulder. "Finish your sprinkles. I'll be fine."

Waving good-night to the lingerers, she left the drugstore and headed back toward the library parking lot, five blocks away. Her jeans felt so tight, she decided to undo the top snap. The relief was instantaneous. Inhaling the crisp night air, she pulled her jacket closer about her shoulders. Stars were everywhere, like sugar sprinkles on chocolate syrup.

The analogy made her smile fade. Funny, she'd never thought of the night sky as chocolate, before. And she'd never had to unbutton her jeans in order to breathe before, either. She wondered idly just what her cholesterol level was, right now? Forty trillion? Oh, who cared, anyway! she chided herself. *Too many years married to a health nut*, she decided. "Darn you, David!" she muttered.

"Ah, ever in your thoughts, I see."

Gina jerked around to see a broad-shouldered cowboy striding out of the shadows.

"David!" she gasped, startled. "Where did you come from?"

He shrugged his hands into his jeans pockets. "I was taking a walk. Nice night." Peering at her oddly, he asked, "What are you doing out here in the dark?"

"I was at the drugstore. A bunch of us had a party. I ate a huge banana split." Why she'd blurted that, she couldn't imagine. She paused, tensing for his huffy disapproval.

"That's nice," he murmured.

She frowned. *That's nice? Was that all he was going to say? No recriminations? No admonitions? What was with him tonight?*

"Are you going back to the lighthouse?" he queried softly.

"I suppose. And you?" she asked, unable to keep the question at bay.

He shook his head. "Think I'll walk awhile longer." With a brief nod, he strolled on by her. "See you tomorrow."

She stiffened, but refused to turn and confront him. "Fine," she shot back. "Tomorrow."

Paying no attention to her whereabouts, she stomped away. *Fine, fine, fine, fine, fine!* If he preferred solitary walks to coming home, that was just fine with her! With every step her mind angrily shouted that one, insipid word, and it ricocheted painfully around in her head. *Fine, fine, fine, fine, fine!*

It wasn't until she was in front of the drugstore that she realized she was heading in the wrong direction. When she finally got back to her car her jaws ached. That seemed odd, since everything was so damned fine!

WHEN DAVID GOT HOME, Gina was awake. She checked the clock radio beside her bed. Three-thirty. Disturbed by the lateness of the hour, she feigned sleep. His shower seemed to take an eternity. When, at long last, he came out of the bathroom, he was towel-drying his hair, naked. She wondered if he knew she was peeping, and was taunting her with his riveting physical perfection. She tried to remind herself that that perfection came with some pretty debilitating strings attached. Nevertheless, she found herself unable to drag her gaze away, grudgingly watching him through lowered lashes until he flipped off the bathroom light.

She could hear him pad around his side of the bed and climb in. Knowing him as well as she did, she could picture him, nude, lying on his back with his hands cradling his head, his ankles crossed. His eyes would be closed, and his lashes would be draped across stalwart cheekbones, enticingly long and thick. She recalled how she used to awaken him by blowing teasingly across those lashes.

Clamping down on such erotic memories, she rolled to her side and punched her pillow.

"Anything wrong?" came the deep, disembodied voice from beyond the blanket that divided their bed.

"No," she retorted, then thought better of it. With a long exhale, she admitted, "Yes, there is, David."

After a prolonged delay that grated on Gina's nerves, he said, "If you want me to apologize for that kiss tonight, then I'm sorry." .

"No, it's not that...." She rolled to face the blanket and tried to think of a way to form her concerns so that he wouldn't assume that she had any disproportionate interest in him. Which, of course, she *didn't*. "I—it's just that I—" She wavered.

"It's just that you what?" David asked, moving in the bed. It sounded as though he, too, had turned to face the blanket that divided them.

She cleared her throat. "It's just that I—well—" She decided it would be best to dive right in. There was no delicate way to say it. "I hope you're employing safe—sex."

The bed didn't move and David made no further sound for what seemed like a week.

"Did you hear me?" Gina demanded, her voice high-pitched and agitated.

"I heard you," he finally replied, sounding vaguely amused.

The amusement she heard hurt. "Well?" she breathed.

"I assure you, Gina, I've never employed safer sex in my life."

She blanched, half expecting him to deny everything. "Oh—well, good. It's just that I know you're a highly sexual being, and—well—we haven't been. You know."

"Yes, I'm afraid I do," David returned, chuckling. "Gina, I'm gratified by your concern, but I am not having sex with any of the numerous sex goddesses in Maryvale. I can't even say I've been hard-pressed to resist their charms."

"Really?" she asked, surprised to feel a weight lifting from her mind.

"Would you like signed documents from the ladies, themselves?"

"Don't be silly."

"Don't you be silly, then," he chided softly. "I love you. Only you. There are no others."

"Then why the late-night strolls? Don't tell me you were just walking!"

"I think, my love, for a woman with no further interest in a man, you protest too much," he taunted gently. "You still care for me, Gina. Face it."

"*Oh!* The vastness of your ego simply boggles the mind!" she retorted. "I was concerned, that's all. Just go to sleep."

"Good night, sweetheart."

Thoroughly disgusted with his imperturbable conviction that she loved him, and with his irritating evasiveness concerning his whereabouts, she pulled her pillow over her head, hoping to blot out any further contact with him. Even so, she believed him. Her imagination had obviously gotten the better of her. David wasn't sleeping with anyone, though it was obvious Iduna was trying her best. Gina knew it was stupid of her to even concern herself with it, but for some absurd reason, she felt better.

David lay very still, wanting to reach out to her, aching to take her into his arms and prove to her that she was the only woman that meant anything to him. Dammit! Time was running short. He had one more week to convince her to come back with him. The morning after the musical was over, he would have to leave.

He'd regretted losing his temper with her last week, and he'd tried to be less critical of her diet and her clothes, though she'd made it purposely tough. It did seem like a good sign that Gina was concerned about his sex life. If she didn't care at all, she wouldn't give a damn. He would cling to that, for now. Still, even as hard as he'd been trying, he knew he'd lost points with her over that taunting kiss tonight. He'd have to work all the harder to make up for it.

Worried, he frowned into the darkness. Gina seemed determined to become some ghost-chasing nonconformist in ripped jeans and corkscrew hair. She wouldn't fit into his academic circles as she was now. But, somehow, he was less frustrated with her for that than with the scholarly types who had set the arbitrary standards of acceptance at AEI: scientists, mainly, with a liberal mix of literary elitists, all bent on dazzling the world with their lettered verbosity. Many of his colleagues would see the new, bizarre Gina as a traitor to their narrow-minded idea of what higher education was all about.

They would, of course, be too polite to be obvious in their distaste, but they would be condescending and aloof. Gina would never stand it, and she'd leave him—again. And what of his career at AEI? What if Quentin recommended him for university president? It was a chance of a lifetime. But David's envious detractors would point out that if he couldn't clamp down on his own wife, how could he effectively run a university of eight thousand students? He had to admit that they would have a valid point.

He rolled onto his back, draping an arm over his eyes. He had one week—seven short days—to convince her to give all this up and come back with him. Dammit to hell! He wanted his Gina back. How in blazes was he going to get her?

GINA SWIRLED INTO the auditorium. It was dress-rehearsal night and she was wearing her most outlandish outfit yet, procured entirely from the local thrift shop. A lime-colored tank-top strap peeked from beneath a faded and torn pink sweatshirt, its neck cut out so that the gaping fabric hung off one shoulder. Her black Lycra biking shorts were skintight, as were her pink tights. Thick, slouchy tan socks and unlaced hiking boots completed the ensemble. She'd pulled her hair to the top of her head and coiled a strip of burlap around and around it, making her coif look like a volcano spewing curly hair.

She looked around. David was sitting with a group of townspeople, apparently being quite folksy and droll in his adopted role as a visiting Texas cowboy. Gina was still surprised by his ability to fit in with the simple folk of Maryvale. She'd thought he would be pompous and superior. She had to give the devil his due. He could act like a "regular guy" when he wanted to. And she had to give him credit in another area, too. During the past five days, he'd been admirably reticent about condemning or poking fun at what she ate, how she dressed or the subject matter of her book.

David had been in the middle of a sentence when he'd chanced to glance in her direction to see her standing there in her oddball regalia. His thick, silky eyebrows lifted in surprise as he looked her over. The pause was long enough for several in the group to follow his gaze. There was unmistakable dismay in David's eyes, but he managed to smile and nod at her.

With an offhand wave, she turned away, but she was unable to dismiss his unhappy look. A sudden, remarkable sadness enveloped her at the memory. With a few glaring exceptions, David had mellowed these last four weeks. Could it be that he was giving up, but was abhorrent to admit it to himself, yet? Could he possibly be slowly, unconsciously, distancing himself from her emotionally? She hoped so—she guessed. *Guessed, nothing!*

she reminded herself grimly. Hadn't that been exactly what she'd been working toward?

And now the whole messy business was almost over. There was tonight's rehearsal, tomorrow night's performance, and then, David would have to go. His precious Albert Einstein Institute and all its stodgy ramifications awaited.

Thirty minutes later, Gina was wearing her blue-and-white calico dress, with eyelet lace edging the puffed sleeves and scoop neckline. She'd tamed her curls with a curling iron, and now her hair fell in soft waves. Parted in the middle, it was pulled back and tied with a ribbon at her nape. As she looked at her reflected image, she was amazed at how different she appeared as Laurey—prim and innocent. Her wide green eyes, no longer obscured by wild wisps of hair, seemed as big as saucers.

A knock sounded at her dressing-room door. "Five minutes, Laurey. And remember, we've got an audience—a busload from the senior citizens' home and some kids from the hospital."

"Okay, Fred," she called, suddenly all nerves. "I'm ready."

The orchestra was tuning up, and she concentrated on the discordant sounds, pushing thoughts of David from her mind. Marjorie had given up her job as accompanist a few days ago. The Maryvale Philharmonic, a twelve-piece orchestra, had belatedly received their music, which had been lost in the mail. From the unappetizing sounds they were generating, Gina felt sure that they could have used another week or two to practice—quite possibly, a decade.

The overture began with a thudding crash of drums, signaling the start of the play. The ensemble sounded tinny and not wholly on key, but no one would complain. The production was for a good cause—Maryvale's community chest. Everyone in town either participated or attended, making several thousand dollars each year for local charitable causes—not to mention the goodwill of tonight's free performance for the area's elderly and convalescent kids.

As Auntie Eller hastened to her place center stage, she threw Gina a kiss for luck. Gina lifted crossed fingers and whispered loudly, "Break a leg!" She inhaled deeply. Trying to calm her nervous stomach, she crept timorously to the wings. The curtain was opening. Auntie Eller busied herself at her butter churn while the overture died away.

It's for a good cause. I'll do fine, Gina promised herself sternly. Wiping her damp hands on her skirt, she hoped she wouldn't disgrace herself and faint.

"Nervous?" came a familiar voice from behind her.

Gina nearly leaped from her skin. With a hand going to her pounding heart, she veered around to see David flash her a teasing grin. He loomed there in a fawn-colored shirt, wide-brimmed cowboy hat and close-fitting jeans. He was the image of the mythical American Cowboy—untamed and unattainable. Not sure why, she took a defensive step backward. "David, you almost gave me a heart attack."

The teasing light had faded from his gaze, and he just stared.

"What?" she asked, noticing the sorrow in his expression. "What's the matter?"

"Nothing." His voice was strangely thick. Slowly and with what seemed like some difficulty, he lifted long fingers to smooth back a stray strand of her hair. "There. Now you're perfect."

"Laurey," Fred called in a hoarse whisper. "Your cue's coming up."

She spun around, tense, trying to prepare mentally for her entrance. Unthinking, she reached up and touched the place David had so recently brushed with his fingers. She recalled his eyes. They had spoken volumes. Costumed as Laurey, he'd seen a glimpse of the old Gina—the sweet, obedient, receptive Gina—and it had hit him hard.

"Go on, Gina," Fred rasped anxiously, with a nudge on her shoulder. "That's your cue."

She stumbled forward, reciting her perky line by rote, for her mind was on David. She'd been married to him so long, she knew instinctively that he hadn't really faced how irrevocably things had changed—not until this minute—not until he'd seen, in Laurey, the Gina he'd lost.

It was ironic that this costume had been the only one Gina had worn without a calculating desire to aggravate David. Yet, this costume was the one that had broken his heart.

12

THOUGH DAVID PLAYED his part as Curly with as much rakish charm as Gina had ever seen it played, she was constantly aware of the unhappiness in his eyes. Even his kisses, when his part required that he kiss her, were subdued.

As the curtain fell after the finale, and the curtain calls were finished, Gina turned to thank David for his reluctance to cause her further mental trauma. But he was gone.

As the other cast members gathered around to congratulate and hug each other for a dress rehearsal well done, Gina searched the shadowed recesses of the wings. Where had he gone so suddenly?

"Heck," groused Paul, "I hope I don't trip over that darned cardboard horse tomorrow night."

"I hope you don't, either," declared Iduna, sounding put out. "At least, if you do, let go of my hand so I don't go down with you. I broke a nail."

"Considering the fact that you two are the play's comic relief, I doubt if anybody realized it was a mistake," Fred offered jovially. "All in all, people, it went great. Now, go on home and get some rest. Tomorrow's the big night." He turned to grab Gina's hand as she started to go. "Just a sec, kid," he said, his expression going serious. "Where's Curly?"

Gina shrugged helplessly. "Disappeared as soon as the curtain fell."

Fred's brows knit.

"Why? Anything wrong?"

He patted her arm. "Naw. I wanted to tell him he did a real convincing job tonight, especially during the scene when he asks you to marry him and you ask him why you should. When he says, 'Cain't ya think of a reason?' I'd have sworn there were tears in that man's eyes." Gina flinched, but said nothing as Fred went on. "What an actor! If he ever wants to give up physics, I think he could make it in Hollywood. He's got looks and—and something else—"

"Charisma?" Gina suggested helpfully, feeling more and more depressed.

Fred snapped his fingers and nodded. "Exactly. It's a rare quality. Well, tell him he did great." Seeming to have a sudden thought, he added hastily, "And you did great, too."

She smiled wanly. "Thanks, Fred. And I'll tell David."

He seemed to want to say something else. Finally, giving into his urge, he asked cautiously, "What is it with you two, anyway? I know it's not my business, but you're both nice kids. Can't you get back together?"

Wishing the whole town didn't know her business, Gina shook her head. "'Fraid not. We want different things out of life."

Fred leaned back on his heels and exhaled tiredly. "Yeah. I hear that happens a lot these days." He shook his head. "Seems like a waste, to me. But who am I to judge? Been married twice myself." He looked at her kindly. "It's a shame. You two seemed to have something nice together." He paused, a slow, sheepish grin blossoming on his face. "When you're not shoving each other off the stage or doing mouth-to-mouth combat. Lordy, what poker-hot passions you two share! I'd give a lot to have one relationship that intense."

She laughed, but it was sad and ironic. "No, you wouldn't, Fred. Trust me."

"Is it true that Curly's leaving after the performance tomorrow night?" he asked, still looking concerned.

"Yes, but where did you hear about it?"

"Iduna. The cast party is going to be a sort of combination cast/goodbye-David party. Didn't you know? Idi took up a collection for a gift."

Gina exhaled raggedly. "I suppose she figured I wouldn't want to contribute."

Fred's brows rose contemplatively. "Maybe. She's sort of acted like she has a thing for the man."

"Yes. She's not very subtle." Hoping Fred would get the message that she was beat, Gina rubbed her nape.

"Sorry, kid," he apologized. "I'll let you go. Good night."

"See you tomorrow, Fred," she murmured, turning away.

By the time she'd removed her makeup and changed out of her costume, everyone was gone. She'd heard some of the people talking about meeting at the drugstore for a little post-dress-rehearsal party, but she didn't feel like partying.

"Hey, Gina," came a cigarette-roughened voice. Too tired to deal with Max, she reluctantly turned. He was grinning at her, his ever-present butt dangling from his lower lip. "Want to go out for a beer?"

Running a hand through her hair, she shook her head. "I'm tired. Not tonight."

Undeterred, he grinned, "Come on. Do you good."

She frowned, eyeing him squarely. "Don't you find the fact that you lift weights to improve your body and still smoke those nasty things a little incompatible?"

He took a drag. "I don't know. Why don't we go somewhere and talk about it."

Shaking her head at him, she persisted, "Some other time. A fog's coming in, and it's going to make the roads bad. See you tomorrow."

"I live close by. No foggy roads."

Striking out past him, she retorted, "Good night, Max."

The drive back was silent and spooky. Fingers of fog drifted across the road, swelling and thickening as she progressed toward her home. It wasn't until she finally reached the lighthouse that the fog had grown impenetrable. Making her way to the door was an eerie sensation, like being lost in a bowl of gray whipped cream. It worried her that David's car wasn't there. The curvy mountain roads weren't particularly conducive to driving blind. And the situation was getting worse by the minute.

David never came home, and Gina couldn't sleep at all, thrashing in her bed, then pacing the floor, harboring horrible visions of his car plunging off into a gorge while groping through the fog.

At four in the morning, she called the Maryvale sheriff's office to ask if there'd been any accidents reported. They told her there hadn't but they'd watch for his car when they made their rounds.

She waited, in bed, hardly breathing, until almost seven, hugging Lumper to her breast, expecting the phone to ring, expecting to be told that her husband was dead. But the call didn't come. Finally, she forced herself to get up, to eat.

As she finished scrambling into a pair of warm-ups, the jangling of the phone startled her, making her cry out as though she'd been struck. Gathering her tattered wits, she ran to the phone, dropping in a huddled lump to the couch before grabbing up the receiver. "Hello," she whispered, her voice husky with fear.

"Mrs. Baron? This is Sheriff Hooligan."

"Yes, sheriff?"

"Er—my deputy, Arnie, just called in to report he's located that rental Mercedes of your—of Dr. Baron's."

Gina's throat constricted. "Is he okay?"

"Yeah. It's parked at the inn. Probably didn't want to drive on those twisting roads in the fog and decided to say there. Well—uh, if that's everything?"

"Yes . . ." she managed, her lips trembling with relief. "Thank you, sheriff. Goodbye." *Of course.* David was too sensible to drive in such a thick fog. Why didn't she think of that? He'd been her sensible, responsible husband for ten years! She should have known that he would have done the sane thing. Right now, though, she wanted to strangle him. Didn't he know she would be worried sick? He should have had the decency to call.

The phone clicked in her ear, and she replaced the receiver. Even her frustration over David's hesitancy to call her didn't overshadow her relief that he was all right. Now that her thoughts were cleared of visions of his crumpled and bleeding body at the bottom of some gorge, her mind turned to a nagging truth she'd discovered during the long, frightening night—a horrible reality she'd been forcefully suppressing.

David was going to be hard to forget, hard to replace. He might be intensely controlling and extremely controlled, but he was an exceptional man. A man of strength, intelligence and compassion—and utterly delicious passions. How could she ever, completely, rid her heart of his hold on it?

What would her life be like tomorrow, when David was gone? What would her hard-fought freedom bring her?

True, she would be able to make all her decisions, but what of her inevitable moments of insecurity? Would there ever again be someone so willing to put aside his work to offer a comforting arm, to share a peaceful sunset, to laugh with her, though no words had been said? Would there ever be anyone else who would work so hard, demand so much of himself, just to give her comfort and security?

"Oh—if only you could find it in you to compromise. Give me some space, a chance to be your partner—your equal..." she cried aloud, drawing a concerned *meow* from Lumper. As the cat bounded into her lap and began to lick her trembling chin, she mumbled, "I—love you, David. I don't want to lose you. Why can't you *help* me...?"

DURING THE FIFTEEN- minute intermission of Saturday night's performance of *Oklahoma*, there was a knock on Gina's dressing-room door. The play was going fine, so far, but Gina had been walking through her part in a strange, numbed state. She was apprehensive about looking David in the eye, and in every scene they'd shared, she'd avoided doing so. She felt frightened, depressed. Time was slipping so quickly away.

Her heart began to pound against her rib cage as the knock sounded again. She didn't know if she wanted it to be David or not. Her hands shaking, she went on dusting her haggard face with powder, hoping to better hide the dark circles below her eyes. "Come in," she called. It had come out as a fragile squeak.

Watching the reflection of the door opening in the makeup mirror, she was a little letdown to see Paul standing there in his chaps, sequined cowboy shirt and wide-brimmed hat, looking as sweet and ineffectual as ever. She smiled, but without much happiness. "Hi." Working at lifting her mood, she teased, "I noticed you had that cardboard horse tamed tonight."

He blushed and grinned at her, pulling a folding chair away from the wall. Turning it to face him, he straddled it, clutching its back with his hands. When he eyed her directly, his smile faded. "You look terrible."

She fumbled with a tube of lipstick. "Thanks," she returned dejectedly. "You should give the halftime pep talks to professional football teams—the ones you want to lose, that is."

He chuckled, but it had a dark, worried sound. "No, Gina, I mean it. What's wrong?"

She shook her head and applied the lipstick before answering. "I didn't sleep well last night."

"Did it have anything to do with David?"

Her hand began to shake so, she had to put the lipstick down. With a sad sigh, she nodded.

"I thought so. What's he done now?"

She lifted a shoulder helplessly. "He didn't come home. Worried me sick. I thought he'd been killed, but the sheriff's office told me his car was parked at the Maryvale Inn."

Another voice, sharp and angry, interjected, "From what I hear, that thoughtless bum's treated you like dirt ever since he got here!"

Both Gina and Paul spun toward the entrance. Max was standing there. He closed the door at his back and lounged against it. In his Jud costume, unshaven and disheveled, he looked every inch a vengeful villain. And there was a vehemence in his eyes that frightened Gina.

With a crude oath, he growled, "Somebody ought to take that smartass bigmouth down a peg or two."

Gina jumped out of her chair and Paul reflexively leaped up as she cried, "Don't you do anything, Max. You shouldn't have been listening. Besides," she added, trying to defuse the situation, "it really shouldn't matter to me. He's leaving me alone, like I asked him to. It's just that with the fog—"

"Don't you see? That crud's gettin' back at you for dumping him."

There was another rap on the door, and Fred's voice called cheerily, "Two minutes, Laurey."

"Okay," she answered, Max's bad-mouthing having set her teeth on edge. "Max, forget—"

"Don't worry, honey, I'll show that big-deal jackass he can't get away with jerkin' you around!" Max ground out. Then, as abruptly as he'd come, he left.

Gina grasped Paul's hand. "Go stop him, Paul. I don't want trouble."

Paul made a sour face and shook his head. "I don't know if I can, Gina. Max's been spoiling for a fight ever since David made a fool of him at rehearsal. Besides, I half want to see that husband of yours get beat up, too. You know how I feel about you."

She squeezed his hand appealingly, her eyes filling. "Please, Paul. David's no match for Max." At her anguished plea, he grimaced. "Okay. I'll try to talk some sense into him."

She managed a sorry smile. "Thanks." Then, wistfully, she added, "If it only could have been you, Paul—you're such a sweet guy."

He snorted in self-disgust. "Yeah, I know. And babies love me, too." He exhaled heavily. "I'll try to catch Max. Besides, you need to get ready." Quickly, and without warning, he dropped a brief kiss on her cheek. "Don't you worry. I'll do my best."

When he had gone, Gina felt worse. She didn't know what Paul's "best" might be, but she had a nagging feeling it wouldn't be good enough.

She shouldn't have said anything. In any case, she certainly hadn't meant for Max to hear. He already had a chip on his shoulder as far as David was concerned. The last thing in the world she wanted was a confrontation between those two. Max would kill him! What she wanted—needed—was a confrontation between herself and David—an air-cleaning to settle things, once and for all. But so far, that just hadn't happened.

David had acted strangely this evening. He'd played his part with a dashing allure she couldn't disregard, drawing her into his loving embrace, smiling at her, teasing, taunting, courting. But offstage, he was quiet, pensive and reserved when they chanced to meet.

Apparently the time for talking about compromises was past. She ran trembly hands over her eyes and inhaled deeply, the scent of grease paint and powder assailing her nostrils. Glancing up, she saw the reflection of a very unhappy woman in the mirror. Closing her eyes, she blocked out the bleak reflection.

The overture started, signaling the beginning of the third act. Grabbing up her bonnet, she scurried out the door to her place in the wings. David was already there. She didn't think he knew she was behind him, but he whispered, "I need to talk to you later, Gina."

She was startled, and suddenly both hopeful and apprehensive. "Talk about what?"

He half turned, his eyes obscured by his hat brim, but his mouth was set in a firm line, his jaw flexing. "It won't take long. Are you going to the cast party?"

"I don't think so."

"Just for a minute?" he urged.

She looked away, not wanting to confront his face—so solemn, yet so splendidly carved it made her heart leap. "I'd rather not."

"Meet me in the parking lot, then?"

She heard her cue. There was no more time to discuss it. Not knowing what else she could do, she hurried past him, but felt him grasp her hand. "The parking lot," he insisted. It hadn't been a question.

"Yes, *yes*, David," she hissed below her breath. "I've got to go."

He released her then, and she ran onstage.

GINA AND DAVID were perched high on a prop haystack. The scene took place late at night, as Curly and Laurey's friends had trapped them up there as a joke during their shivaree. This was the climactic scene where Jud, in his jealousy and twisted need for revenge, decides to burn Curly and Laurey alive as they are alone and isolated atop the hay.

Gina was serious. There had been a malevolent glint in Max's eyes ever since he'd overheard her talking to Paul about David's not returning home. And now that look was all too evident as David, unaware of Max's animosity, made his leap from the hay to thwart Jud's evil plan. The two men began to scuffle, as they were supposed to do. But a few seconds into the choreographed fracas, Gina heard Max mumble, "Think fast, Doc," slamming David in the face with a right cross. Caught off guard, David staggered backward in surprise.

Gina screamed, then covered her mouth, remembering the audience. "No—don't—" she cried, hoping Max would relent. After all, the script required that David *win* this fight.

Max leered at David as he reeled back. "How'd you like that, Mr. High-and-Mighty?" he challenged under his breath, advancing again.

David stared at Max, stunned. Shaking his head to clear his vision, he touched his nose. It was bleeding. "Are you crazy?" he accused, in just above a whisper.

"Let's say I'm followin' an uncontrollable urge." He took another shot, clipping David's jaw, and he stumbled backward, again.

Gina cast a helpless glance around. Everyone in the cast was crowded in the wings, looking aghast. Fred was wiping his brow, his expression alarmed.

Cautiously they circled each other. Gina shot a frightened glance toward the audience. They were caught up in rapt attention, unaware that the fight onstage was real.

She bit into her finger, struggling mentally. What could she do? David was no match for Max. He was no fighter. He wasn't even defending himself! She tried again, pleading as inaudibly as she could, "Don't hurt him—Ma—Jud!"

Max lunged, plugging David with a hard shot to the solar plexis. Gina cried out. Fred dropped his script and stomped on it.

Doubled over, David saw stars. He couldn't breathe and he tasted blood. Shuffling backward, he sucked in some air, but not enough. What the hell had come over Max? It surely had something to do with his obsession for Gina, but he didn't know what could have made the man go insane like this.

When he'd managed to partially straighten, Max was right there, landing a left to his cheek. The force of it spun David around. Though he lurched badly, he managed to keep from falling, but not by much.

There was a gasp from the audience as they rooted for their hero. Right now, Curly didn't feel much like a hero. He felt more like a punching bag. What in the hell was he going to do?

A bit disjointedly, he reeled back to face Max. "Damn it, man," he forced out through a groan. "What's your problem?"

"I wanted Gina to see you for the *zero* you are. Thanks for not disappointing me," he jeered. With a disgusted snort, he ground out, "Let's get this farce over with."

At long last, Max pulled his rubber knife from his boot and charged David. The rehearsed tussle lasted for another few minutes before Max belatedly did as he was supposed to do. With a high-pitched cry of pain, he fell on his fake knife and feigned death.

The play ended in a daze for Gina, still in a state of shock at having to watch David take such a beating. She felt sick at heart. It had been her fault.

Luckily, David had been offstage long enough for one of the stagehands, a first-aid-course graduate, to clean up his bloodied nose. When the two combatants passed each other in the wings as David was about to go back onstage, Max shot him a belligerent look. "If it weren't for the show, I'd have laid you out, man."

David halted, turned and watched Max huff away. Shaking his head, and then grimacing at the pain it caused, he put the ice pack back on his cheek to wait for his cue. Was he nuts or was the whole mess a bad dream?

When the curtain finally fell and David released Gina from a kiss that had been understandably tentative, considering his sore face, he asked, "Why did Max try to kill me?" His voice a harsh rasp, he went on, "I'm sure you know, because I'm only in pain when you're involved."

Feeling guilty over her unintentional responsibility, but unable to admit, she stormed, "That's not fair, David. I didn't want him to hurt you. He had to know it wouldn't be a fair fight."

A cold smile suddenly lifted his lips, and he softly accused, "You really do think I'm a coward, don't you?"

She cast her gaze away, hoping she thought no such thing. But she couldn't help saying, "David—any man has the right to defend himself."

He grunted out a bitter laugh. "Maybe. Maybe not." Taking her by the arm and aiming her toward her dressing room, he ordered, "Change. I'll meet you in the parking lot in twenty minutes."

"Are you going to be all right?" she asked, worriedly scanning his bruised profile.

He turned, capturing her gaze with his grave, steady observation. "I'll know that soon enough," he murmured, before pivoting away.

She watched him disappear around a corner, wondering what he'd meant. Perplexed and feeling thoroughly drained, she entered her dressing room.

Fifteen minutes later, she'd changed into her faded sweatpants and orange sweatshirt. Her hair fell in soft waves halfway to her waist, the curling iron having stolen the wildness from her curls. When she reached the dark parking lot, David wasn't there, but Max appeared silently, as though he'd been waiting for her.

She stiffened, granting him an indignant frown. "How *could* you, Max?" she demanded. "How could you have done that to David, and right onstage?"

He leaned against the hood of his midsize sedan and half grinned. "Don't be mad at me, Gina. The guy needed to be taught a lesson, so I taught him one. End of story." He held out a hand, taking her by the elbow. "I had a feeling you weren't going to stay for the cast party. So, what do you want to do? I'm free all night." It had come out sounding suggestive.

She withdrew her arm from his grasp. "I'm going no-where with you. You proved nothing with your display of temper except that you can throw your weight around. David doesn't even know why you hit him."

"Right. Sure. He's a smart Ph.D. He'll figure it out." Taking her arm again, he insisted, "Come on." He led her to the passenger door of his car. "We'll go to my place and celebrate the play's success and the fact that David's leaving. I bought some good wine—"

She jerked away, highly irritated. "Max, I hope you're not deluding yourself into believing you beat David up for me, because you didn't. You did it because you're jealous of him."

Max turned abruptly, his face hardening. "You're kidding," he retorted in disbelief.

She shook her head, adamant. "I've tried to be civil to you, but you've been an irritant in my life from the first moment we met. You're a small man, Max. You have to build up your ego by making other people seem smaller than you. You decided you wanted me, so you had to try and make David look inadequate in my eyes. But you only made yourself look bad. Even bruised and bleeding, David's a better man than you are. Everybody in town likes him, and you can't stand that—can't stand not being the coolest dude around!"

"Even *you* like him, I suppose?" he demanded.

She wanted to look away, but she forced herself to eye him directly. "I'm not happy about it, but—yes. I like him. There's a lot of goodness and kindness in David Baron."

His features contorted in a scowl. "Don't you see why I had to do what I did? I'm crazy about you, babe," he admitted pleadingly, grasping her by the shoulders. "You've been my one-and-only fantasy since that time I saw you flounce out of your house buck naked. Don't brush me off.

Give me a chance. I'm a great guy when you get to know me."

She reached up to dislodge his painful grip from her shoulders. "That—that hurts. I'd like to go ho—"

"Not on your life!" he spat. "You've been teasing me and leading me around by the nose for two weeks now, honey. And those kisses onstage? I know you were *supposed* to be fighting me off, but, hell, they weren't cold-fish stuff. You were telling me things with those kisses." Gina's eyes widened as he raged on, "Come on, sweet thing, deep down, you wanted the old doc beat up. You just picked the wrong dude. Paul being the wimp he is, I figured I had to step in. And now that you got what you wanted, you're giving me the boot? No way! You're coming with me."

She slapped him hard across the face and spun away to escape, but he caught her arm. "Come on, babe," he whined. "I'm sorry, just lost my head for a minute. Look, I've made plans—a late dinner—steaks, caviar. It'll be fun." Dragging her back, he fumbled for the latch on his car door, bent on getting her inside.

"Let go of me, Max!" she cried.

"I'd do as the lady asks," a deep voice boomed from behind them.

The redhead craned around to see David looming there. Gina could see him, too. Even damaged as he was, he looked darkly forbidding. His eyes, like liquid mercury, held a lethal glint.

Gina's heart began to hammer with fear—but not for herself; for him. She'd caused David enough physical punishment for one night, and she knew Max was in an ugly mood. Frightened for him, she exclaimed, "David, stay out—"

Max's harsh laugh cut her off. "Well, well. If it isn't Mr. Turn-the-Other-Cheek. Go lead a peace march somewhere, man. This isn't your business."

David's nostrils flared. "Are you going to let her go?"

"Max," Gina cried, "don't start anything else! David's already hurt."

"I won't hurt little David anymore," Max sneered. "Let's get out of here." He opened the door and with a hard grip on Gina's arm, forced her into the seat.

"Do you want to go with him, Gina?" David asked, his voice tightly controlled.

"No," she stated. "I'm going home." When she attempted to get out, Max closed the door, imprisoning her inside.

"Move along, Baron. Gina and I are going to have a quiet little talk."

"Not while you're in this mood, friend," David warned, clamping a halting hand down on Max's shoulder. "Get out, Gina."

When she unlatched the door, Max shot angrily, "Get your paw off of me!" Punching away David's hand, he snarled, "Okay, you asked for it, pal!"

The redhead hauled back a fist that looked powerful enough to lay David flat. A scream of panic rose in Gina's throat. Eyes wide, she watched, frozen in horror, as Max's fist rocketed forward toward David's injured face.

But the impact never came. David blocked Max's punch. With authority, he grabbed Max's arm and stepped deftly behind him, pinning his arm at an angle so unnatural it made Gina blanch. With his free hand, David grasped Max by the hair at his temple, making him howl a second time.

"I think I've had enough," David began, his words edged with menace. "How about you, *pal?*"

"Dammit, Baron," Max complained through clenched teeth, "you're breaking my arm."

"No, I'm not. I could, but I'm not." His face a striking study in controlled fury, he admitted grimly, "You see, I hit a man once. Blinded him. Vowed I'd never hurt another person." Gina watched in stunned silence as David's features twisted at the memory. "But for you, Max, I could almost make an exception." Cocking his head at Gina, he ordered softly, "Get out of the car."

She scrambled out and hurried beyond Max's reach. When she'd done so, David maneuvered the brawny man around to the driver's side. The trip was difficult for Max, arched back painfully and forced to walk on his toes. His head was pulled to one side, and his expression told a tale of misery. "Hell, man, *I'm going.*"

Releasing the sensitive hair above Max's ear, David opened the car door and with a helpful shove, delivered him inside. "Good night, then, Murphy. Sleep well."

He shot David a murderous glare. "Man, I've never hated anyone like I hate you."

David grinned maliciously down at him. "What a shame. And I was about to ask you to the prom." Straightening, he thrust the door shut and stepped back, narrowly missing having his toes flattened by Max's retreating car.

When the redhead had gone, he left behind only the odor of burned rubber. Knowing that in his anger at Max he'd lost his hard-fought control and said too much, David reluctantly glanced over at Gina. She was staring, her lips parted in amazement. The time had come to dredge up old hurts he'd hoped were buried forever.

In a strained whisper, she asked, "What did you mean when you said you blinded someone?"

He averted his gaze, his features going cold as Gina watched wordlessly. He didn't answer or move. He just stood there: so tall, so devastatingly attractive, so damaged—and, suddenly, a complete enigma. Closing the distance between them, she gently touched his wounded cheek. "David," she whispered sadly, "I'm so sorry about this. But you could have stopped it. You did—just now."

"No. I couldn't."

She was confused. "Why?"

He faced her again, his expression grim. "I made a promise to myself."

"You mean you really blinded someone?" she asked in disbelief.

He glanced up at the starry sky and exhaled slowly, heavily. The torture etched on his features was answer enough.

"Who, David?"

When their gazes clashed again, moisture was glistening on his lower lashes. In a whisper that was fierce and full of self-loathing, he said, simply, "My father."

13

"YOUR FATHER?" she said with disbelief.

"I don't want to talk about it, Gina. It's ancient history."

She shook her head. "No, David. I must know."

He dropped his fists into his slacks pockets. "Would you mind if we did this somewhere else, then?"

She scanned the parking lot, having forgotten her whereabouts. "Let's go home."

They both took their own cars. The twenty-minute drive seemed like a year. All she could think about was David blinding his father and being so strongly affected by the experience that he'd vowed never to lift a hurtful hand again, not even to defend himself. Her mind raced and stumbled over itself, her thoughts pouncing on various ways he might have harmed his father—it was certainly an accident. David wasn't a violent person. He had shown himself to be a man with a temper, though he usually kept it tightly in check. And he wasn't a man to purposely harm anyone—especially his own father.

Once they were both inside the lighthouse and Gina had fixed a pot of strong coffee, they took their usual places on separate sides of the kitchen table. Gina prodded softly, "Tell me about your father, David."

A spasm of self-hatred passed across his face. He'd lifted his mug halfway to his lips. Without drinking, he lowered it to the table.

Gina said nothing more. She merely watched him, scanned his anguished expression. Lumper jumped into his lap, and she noticed that he absently began to stroke the cat's back. When he finally spoke, his voice was strangely devoid of emotions, "My father was a Texas oil wildcatter for twenty years, until he struck it rich at forty. My mother was a frail woman, two years older than Dad." He paused, his lips thinning. "My father drank, and when he got drunk, he hit my mother."

Gina gasped. Pulling her lips between her teeth, she forced herself to keep still and listen.

"They didn't have me until my mother was forty-four. I was just a kid, but I remember hearing her cry, seeing her bruises. For a long time, I didn't understand. My folks were wealthy, pillars of the Dallas community, but my mother had to wear long sleeves, high collars and sunglasses to her women's clubs, to hide the fact that she was abused. Thinking back on it, I doubt if she fooled anyone, but in those years, people figured it wasn't anybody's business if a man beat his wife."

He stopped again. An angry muscle began to jump in his jaw as his memories became more vivid. Gina's heart went out to him and she reached across the dividing tape to cover his hand with hers. "Please—go on."

"When—" He cleared his throat and gritted out, "One night just after I'd turned ten, my father came home late. I was awakened by the sound of something hitting the wall in my parents' room. I ran down the hall and when I opened their door, I realized it had been my mother who'd been slammed into it. She was whimpering, slumped on the floor, her arms up to protect her face as my father slapped her around." He withdrew his hand from Gina's, as though, by his mere relationship to his abusive father, he wasn't worthy of being comforted.

"What happened?" Gina inquired softly, her voice catching in her throat.

"I went crazy. Ran screaming at my father, jumped him and started hammering him with my fist. He was drunk, and with me hanging on his neck, he staggered and fell. Hit his head on the bedpost and went down hard." David cast her a stricken look. The loathing that had crossed his features returned, settled there, marring it. He closed his eyes, whispering hoarsely, "When he woke up, he was blind.

"He hated my guts after that, but at least he was no longer a threat to my mother. She sent me off to England to avoid the media scandal, and, she hoped, to help me forget. Dad cut me out of the will. Six months later, reeling drunk, he fell down the stairs and broke his neck."

Gina's eyes filled with tears as he finished roughly, "He'd left everything to Mother, for once doing something good for her. Mother's will left it all to me. She died of lung cancer when I was thirteen—she'd been a heavy smoker." His lips twisted in a sad smile. "Her one vice—besides loving my father."

Gina frowned in thought. No wonder David was so controlled and so health-conscious. His father had been an abusive drunk and David had probably reasoned he could end up that way, too. And his poor mother, dying so horribly. . . .

He took a slug of coffee, then looked in her direction, but his gaze was faraway. He was seeing something in some other place, distant and long ago. Finally he said, "The headmaster at Harthrow was a devotee of martial arts. He knew about my dad, and about my aversion to violence. There was a boy at our school who was legally blind without his glasses and a frail young man with a withered arm. Headmaster put the three of us in a special class. We never had to do the punching and kicking karate involved. We were only taught self-defense maneuvers in line with our abilities. I was physically able, but emotionally unwilling, at first. After a while, he convinced me to take part, by telling me I could thwart violent acts with self-defense training." He lifted his big, expressive hands, and for a moment, just stared at them. "I didn't think I'd remember, all these years later."

Placing Lumper on the floor, he stood. "Now you've seen the slimy underbelly of David Baron's childhood. Pretty, isn't it?"

She hurried to her feet. Crossing the dividing line, she took him into her arms and placed her cheek on his chest. "I'm so sorry about your mother and father. But you mustn't blame yourself."

"I've been told that." She could hear the powerful beat of his heart, and with her comforting closeness, its pace quickened. He placed his hands on her arms and gently separated them. "I never told you all this, Gina, because I never wanted your pity." Solemnly he reminded her, "But there is something we need to talk about."

She was drawn back to the reality of their situation by his intent stare. "Yes, I suppose there is," she admitted reluctantly, unhappy about the possibility of one last confrontation between them. But, as with anything that is dying or being killed, their marriage had to have its final death throes. "What do you want to talk about?" she queried, her voice as solemn as his had been, though she already knew the answer.

"Us, of course." His expression told her he knew she was stalling.

She swallowed hard. "Is there an 'us'?" Her heart fluttered with a tangle of unwelcome emotions: dread, hope, compassion—and unquenchable love.

A sad smile flitted across his face, softening his features. "As far as I'm concerned there always will be an 'us,' Gina. Don't you know that?"

She shook her head sadly. "How could I, when you didn't even bother to let me know you weren't dead last night. When you never came home, I had to call the sheriff to find that out."

He stared, incredulous. "You were worried about me?"

She stared back, equally incredulous. "How could you even ask?"

He chuckled sadly. "Well—perhaps it's the fact that you've been telling me to get the hell out of your life for a month."

She blanched, feeling something twist in her gut. "Is that what you were doing—getting out of my life?"

A flash of pain darkened his features. With an inclination of his head, he indicated the living room. "Could we sit?"

She nodded. Her legs were suddenly wobbly, and it was almost imperative that she sit down.

With a gesture that told her to precede him, she led the way.

He followed close behind her, murmuring, "I love you, Gina."

She grew fearful, self-protective. She couldn't allow him to cajole his way back into her life and her bed—not until some big changes were made. "Don't do this, David," she pleaded, her tone going defensively stern. Dropping to the couch, she tucked her feet beneath her and focused on him as he settled into his easy chair. She felt shaky and frightened. What happened now would affect them for the rest of their lives. "Okay," she continued a bit breathlessly, "is that what you were doing? Were you getting out of my life?"

He sat back, crossing his arms before his chest. His gaze rested on her, steady and watchful. "I needed to be alone— wanted to drive around and think. The fog was bad, so I pulled off the road at Lookout Point. I listened to the pounding of the surf for hours, thinking about you, thinking about the fact that I have to leave. Finally, some- where around four in the morning, I fell asleep."

She was listening intently. When he paused, she prompted, "And?"

"And, I woke up around seven. Fog was worse. I didn't have everything thought out, didn't know what to say to you, so I decided to go back into town, to the inn, take a shower, try to work things out."

She looked down at her lap. She was nervously twid- dling her thumbs. Clamping her hands tightly together, she whispered, "Why didn't you call?"

"I'm sorry about that," he apologized. "I didn't think you gave a damn where I was. And at the time, I didn't know what to say."

"Is that what you've been doing all those nights you've been out so late?"

"Walking, watching the ocean at Lookout Point, or driving. You know I like to drive when I have something to sort out."

"But you never did this much driving."

He shook his head, looking sad. "I never had to figure a way to keep you before. It's been the hardest damn work I've ever done."

She sucked in an apprehensive breath, afraid to ask the question that was trembling on her tongue. She opened her mouth several times, but the words wouldn't come. After a dreadfully long moment, David obliged by asking it for her. "Did I come up with a way? That's what you want to know, isn't it?"

Her throat blocked with emotion, she could only nod.

He rose slowly, his silver gaze holding hers with an intense power that she could not—or would not—fight. As he moved toward her, she could feel her cheeks go hot—whether with apprehension or anticipation, she couldn't fathom. "What—did you decide?" she managed tightly. When he was standing over her, they exchanged a long, silent look.

David, looking supremely sad, slowly shook his dark head. "I only know I can't lose you, Gina." He pulled her up to stand before him. "Without you, I would become like some dry textbook, existing but not alive." He drew her into his arms, kissing first one cheek and then the other, promising huskily, "I'll listen to any suggestions—" he kissed the tip of her nose before finishing "—that you might have."

Gina's mind was clouding with foolish desire for him. His scent was seductive; his words, soft and beguiling; his lips, tempting. She managed to retain enough of her wits to press against his chest and turn her face away, declaring feebly, "David, this isn't—please . . ."

"Tell me, Gina," he coaxed softly, his kisses burning along her jaw. "What will it take to keep you?"

Her head lolled back traitorously, exposing the delicate column of her throat to his sultry exploration. She mouthed the word "Compromise," but no sound came. She tried again. This time, the single word came out in a half croak, half moan.

His hands were working their familiar miracles—massaging, enticing. Gina shook her head to clear it, pressing on his broad chest again. "Did you hear me?"

He kissed the hollow of her throat, "Yes, my love." Lifting her into his arms, he carried her into the bedroom and placed her on the bed. With one strong swipe of his arm, he tore down the rope that divided the bed, and the blanket fluttered across her legs.

Gina sat up abruptly, flinging away the cover to free her legs. She was ready to run when she demanded, "What are you..."

Her words dwindled away in surprise as he followed her quickly down. "I was hoping you might agree to compromise," he whispered.

Startled by his sudden acquiescence, she asked, "Are you saying you will?"

He smiled down at her as he settled himself in a thoroughly scandalous manner that required that she widen her legs. "Of course. I can't lose you."

A thrill rushed through her, swelling her heart. All fear and doubt fell away, and she felt as though she'd been freed from heavy shackles. "Oh, David," she cried, tears filling her eyes. "I never thought you would agree to such a thing. You never compromise."

Curling arms about his neck, she met his kiss eagerly, her mouth slanting across his, open, welcoming and torrid.

He groaned with relief and pleasure. "I love you so much," he murmured, his tongue flicking her lips, her teeth, the tender recess of her mouth, delighting her. "I'd give up everything for you."

Her breasts heaved in growing excitement at the passion he was stirring inside her, both with the wonder of his words and his lips, his hands. He was once again hers— and there was a new openness, equalness, within the relationship. David had actually promised to compromise! He would give up *everything* for her! She was delirious, and with a relish she hadn't known for a long time, she ran her tongue provocatively across his lower lip, nipping playfully. From the position in which he had imprisoned her with his hard, taut body, she could readily detect his arousal, and she giggled with heady anticipation.

He came up on one elbow, smiling down at her, his eyes gleaming like polished silver, his lashes lowered questioningly. "What's so funny?" he asked softly.

"I'm just so happy." She reached up to toy with the top button of his pin-striped shirt.

He sat up, gently brushing her hand away. "No, my love. You first. I want to feast my starving eyes on you."

She felt unexpectedly shy as he began to lift her sweatshirt upward. Their eyes continued to lock, and they smiled at each other, their expressions deeply loving, expectant, intense.

The shirt removed, David caressed the soft flesh of her exposed breasts with his thumb, seductively, unhurriedly. Gina closed her eyes and sighed as his lips replaced his thumb, and she lifted her arms to his head, pressing, caressing his soft curls, pressing his moist, hot mouth more intimately into her softness.

Arching upward, she helped as he removed the scrap of lace that was her bra, and his sensual search resumed as he teased and nipped, drawing gasps of heightened pleasure from her.

In a daze of passion, Gina was relieved of the remainder of her clothes, and David paid ultimate masculine homage to her body. Secret, cloistered places were gently conquered and glorified by the vast expertise of his lips. Engulfed in delicious sensations, she reached for him, clawing, frenzied by a woman's need to draw him into her, to complete the uniting of their bodies, their eternal souls.

When, at last, David became one with her, she allowed herself an unabashed moan of joy and circled his powerful hips with her legs. She wanted to hold him within her intimate grasp for an endless time. But David had other ideas. He thrust deeply against her, drawing a cry of pleasure.

With a low chuckle and a lingering kiss, he murmured, "This is only the beginning, sweetheart...."

They moved together, more and more quickly, their bodies taking on a wild rhythm as their fervor burned higher. Gina held on to David as he thrust sweetly, blessedly, driving her toward the brink of rapture.

Tears of ecstasy ran down her cheeks, and she cried out his name as she plunged into the rending oblivion of her orgasm. Her breathing came in short, ragged gasps, and she found herself crying, sighing, laughing. She was euphoric, fulfilled—and unreservedly in love.

David's release was less exuberant. He stilled above her and clung to her, his body tense, but she could feel his shudder within her, and she delighted in the emotional closeness of the moment, kissing his damp shoulder.

Neither spoke for a long time, simply relishing their harmony of spirit. Finally David stirred, whispering hoarsely, "I didn't dare even dream of this...."

Her heart near to bursting, she stroked his hard, slick back with her fingernails. "Me, neither. I love you so, but I thought I'd taken everything too far for us ever to come back together this way."

As he lifted his head to gaze down at her, his face held an other worldly beauty: eyes glistening between long, dark lashes, tousled curls, strong, masculine lips gentled by their lovemaking. He shook his head at her as if to say she never could have taken things too far. "I will always love you, Gina," he vowed quietly.

Unable to resist the urge to ruffle his hair further, she asked, "So what are you going to do about Al Einstein Institute?"

His expression grew quizzical. "What do you mean?"

She teased a lock of his hair, twirling it around her finger. "I mean, since you're not going back. What will you tell them?"

His expression darkened. "Not going back? Why wouldn't I go back?"

She felt a thread of trepidation snake up her spine. "Naturally, since I told you I can't go back, I assumed you meant you weren't either—when you said you were willing to compromise."

He chuckled at her silliness. "Of course, I'm willing to compromise, darling, but I meant you could wear your hair curly and we'd eat red meat a couple times a week." His smile grew tolerant. "Perhaps even three times, occasionally."

Gina recoiled. Feeling dizzy and disoriented by this unexpected blow, she could do little more than shake her head from side to side, denying it, telling herself she hadn't heard him right. In a tight little voice, she repeated, "Red meat? Curly hair? That's not the compromise you were talking about, is it?"

Confused by her distress, he replied, "Naturally. That's what a compromise is, isn't it?"

Feeling as though she'd been slapped, she struggled from beneath him, backing toward the wall. "David, so far you've done nothing but make noises like a lenient father! Those weren't compromises—they were *crumbs!* I'm not some pigeon you're trying to coax back into a coop, I'm a human being! And I've told you from the beginning, I'm *not* going back to AEI! *I can't!*"

His gaze narrowed, grew foreboding. "Do you mean to tell me that in order to keep you, I can't go back to my work? My profession? That's your idea of a compromise?"

"It has to be that way," she declared helplessly, knowing she was asking too much, knowing he couldn't give her what she wanted, but wishing he would come further than he had—give her something more than scraps. Still damp from their loving, her body began to quake, but more from emotional turmoil than the coolness of the air. This was the deathblow to their marriage she had dreaded—the end.

He shook his head in disbelief. "You're asking me to give up everything."

"*Everything*? And only a short while ago, you said I was everything to you," she reminded him sadly.

He cursed. "Gina, don't make me choose between you and my work. I love my work."

She fought nausea, charging brokenly, "Then go back and make love to it!"

His features contorted in a scowl. "I have to leave today. Are you coming back with me, or not?"

"I—I can't," she cried. "Nothing's changed. Listen to yourself. You're dictating to me again. Good Lord, we're still naked from making love and you're already trying to control me." She scrambled from the bed and stumbled on trembly legs to the bathroom door.

His breath harsh in his throat, he watched her run. Pale, fragilely beautiful, she was struggling away from him, and the pain of it was like a knife in his belly. But David was angry. The little hellion wanted everything her way. She wasn't compromising, either! Before she could close the bathroom door between them, he growled, "Why can't *you* give up a little, compromise a little bit?"

She turned on him, her eyes large, anguished, spitting jade fire. "*A little bit?*" With an utterly devastated sob, she retorted, "Why don't you just go *a little bit* to hell!"

Epilogue

THERE WAS AN AUTUMN crispness in the salt air as September drew to a vivid close. The briny scent of the ocean breeze mixed pleasantly with the smells of the forest. Gina sat with her back supported by the rough bark of a redwood as Lumper entertained himself by bounding among the ferns. It had taken the cat weeks to venture outside at all, and now he would go only if Gina was within pouncing distance. She picked a frond and absently toyed with it, smiling at Lumper's antics while he darted one way and then another, startling insects into flight.

"Just don't startle any snakes or spiders my way," she warned. But Lumper paid no heed, scampering happily about.

She swallowed, her eyes trailing over the sanctity of the woods. She'd spent more and more time out here since David's angry departure a month ago. A sharp pang wrenched her as she recalled him. David's face had been drawn, making the bones of his cheeks and jaw appear even more prominent, and his voice had been devastatingly cool as he said goodbye.

Days later, after she'd wrung herself dry crying, she'd taken to working on her book in the sun-dappled solitude of the forest. There, there were fewer memories, fewer painful distractions. At least her book was going well—

or so her editor had told her after he'd scanned the first six chapters she'd sent him. That was good news.

She sighed heavily. Good news. She supposed so. He'd even sweetened the tidings with an advance check of five thousand dollars. Though Gina lived frugally, the money would certainly come in handy.

"Five thousand dollars will buy a lot of cat food." She smiled wanly. "I hope."

Lumper abruptly bounded into her lap, drawing a grunt from her. "You're getting too fat to do that, fella," she scolded softly, stroking him into a fit of purring. "Maybe I should reconsider the cat food."

The sky was growing dark, and she could no longer work. It was time to go back to the lighthouse—the lonely, empty lighthouse. She sighed again—something she'd been doing all too often lately. She was still grieving over her loss of David. She'd foolishly hoped he'd relent; that he'd write, phone, *something*. But she hadn't heard a word from him.

Another thing she hadn't done was initiate new divorce proceedings. Lord knew why. There was certainly no reconciliation brewing. David had made his choice clear, and so had she. End of marriage.

Still, she hesitated. Every day she expected to hear from his lawyers, but nothing materialized. So she continued to live in a limbo state. It wasn't so bad, really. She had no desire to date, and being legally married was as good an excuse as any to detour interested men.

Closing her spiral notebook, Gina dumped Lumper out of her lap and stood. "It's time to fix dinner. What do you want tonight, Tuna Festival or Sailor's Surprise?"

Lumper rubbed her leg, meowing.

"A can of Tuna Festival, it is. But promise you won't get into my fish if I have to get up from the table to answer the phone. You did last week, remember? I had to eat peanut butter."

Lumper rubbed, turned and rubbed again.

She lifted him in her arms. "Well—I doubt if it'll make much of a problem. I don't believe the siding salespeople will call again quite this soon."

She trudged toward the edge of the wood thinking about her life as it was now. She liked Maryvale, but she lived so far from town, she missed a lot. And her work was terribly solitary. Paul had finally—and sensibly—given up on her, and any other interested men had been gently rebuffed. Max, his macho ego bruised, had not only not called, but had gotten a new parcel-delivery route.

Gina had become involved as a hospital volunteer one day a week, but, all things considered, she was lonesome. And, having gained ten pounds, she was on a diet. She'd learned to abide salads and had found that baked fish seasoned with herbs and lemon was not only tasty but took less work than frying.

If David could only see her now. Allowing herself a sad, ironic smile, she realized she'd even relinquished quite a bit of her outlandish wardrobe to more conventional dress. Deep down, Gina supposed she wasn't a true rebel. She'd rebelled, yes; but it wasn't her nature to be resistant to all social values—just David's narrow concept of them.

She left the wood and headed across the open field toward her lighthouse. Out over the jutting cliff, she could see the explosion of color that boded the end of the day. The sun was diving into the ocean, molten, dying, but not without a bloody fight. The magnificent scene reminded her of the night David had appeared on the beach and tossed their divorce papers into the flames where The Dean's Wife burned. She tried to force the memory from her mind and trod around the corner of the lighthouse and up the path to her porch.

As she opened the door, she thought she smelled smoke drifting up from the sea. *Smoke?*

Curious, she put the cat inside along with her notebook and turned to scan the sea. Nothing. But from this vantage point she couldn't see much of the beach.

Someone must be down there, trespassing. It happened every so often. She usually didn't mind. Nevertheless, she'd have to go down and tell them it was private property and to clean up before they went. Then she'd tell them where a public beach was located. There'd never been any trouble—usually just a couple in love and seeking privacy. Still, every time she had to face the situation, she was a little nervous. These days, one never knew. . . .

When she reached the edge of the cliff, she peered down, unsure what to do next. A bonfire flickered in competition with the grandeur of the sunset. She approached with caution, descending the long, twisting path of steps reluctantly. No one appeared to be attending the fire. *Strange.*

When, at last, she was standing before it, gazing into it almost transfixedly, she heard a sound and turned.

The man stood some twenty feet away, the shadow of a jutting arm of the cliff masking his features. But the set of his broad shoulders and the command in his stance gave him away.

"David . . ." she breathed, her throat suddenly going so dry, she could hardly swallow to clear it.

He began to move forward and she noticed that he was carrying something. When he'd reached the flickering light of the fire, she could tell it was a suitcase. "You look lovely, Gina." His voice came softly, whispered through the gathering shadows.

Her lips opened soundlessly. She was wearing yellow. He detested yellow on her. "What—what are you doing here?" she asked, perplexed.

He regarded her with soft, gray eyes for a long moment. The surf pounded against the shore but Gina could only hear the pounding of her heartbeat. Without preamble, he knelt and opened the suitcase, drawing from it an expensive suit. With a disinterested toss, he sent the suit sprawling into the flames.

Gina sucked in a surprised breath, her eyes widening. "What—are you doing?" she cried, staring blankly at the costly worsted as it became ash and smoke.

He tossed more clothes onto the fire. Only when the suitcase was also a crackling, hissing memory did he move to her side. "Can't you guess?" Some elemental emotion in his silvery eyes stilled the breath in her throat as he murmured, "I'm burning The Dean." He spared his expensive wardrobe the most cursory of glances before he added with a wry grin, "Dastardly bore he was, too. I say, let him burn."

She blinked, stunned. "Really, David?"

He nodded, his smile gentling, his teeth glinting mischievously. "But I'm not through."

She was confused until he slid one suspender off his shoulder, then the other.

"David?" she asked, her voice edged with a mixture of shock and delight. "Are you undressing?"

He flashed that grin again. "Mmm, hmm." The trousers slid tantalizingly down along his muscular thighs.

"But—but what will you do about clothes?" she queried, her eyes feasting on his slow, fire-lit striptease.

"I don't think we'll have to worry about that for days," he suggested, his voice full of sensual promise.

The trousers hit the flames, followed swiftly by his tassel moccasins and designer socks.

Gina watched in awe. "But—but AEI?"

His shirt was slipping open one button at a time, though he kept his eyes on hers. "I told them I needed a year off—maybe more. I had some writing to do, and so did my wife. We'd let them know."

The shirt slid off his broad shoulders, and Gina licked her lips unconsciously as the firelight paid greedy homage to his flesh.

When the shirt fluttered to its demise, he touched her face, whispering, "We could make AEI a better place—more spontaneous, more open and—human. It doesn't have to be stuffy. Maybe someday we can go back?"

Inhaling his familiar scent, she scanned his face, now very solemn. Unable to fathom what was happening, she could only stare. "I don't know what to say," she finally managed, feeling stupid and dull-witted. "This is such a shock. What do your colleagues at AEI think?"

With emotion glistening in his eyes, he confessed, "I don't give a damn what they think." His lips twisted wryly. "After all, once they've seen my wife throw aspic over my head, what could they possibly say? You're delightfully unique, Gina. I need you."

Guiltily, she dropped her gaze. "I shouldn't have asked you to quit your job. It was selfish of me."

"Maybe it was your turn to be selfish," he offered softly. Lowering his head to hers, he gently kissed her lips. The endearment had been so tentative, it had felt like the caress of a butterfly's wing. "Sweetheart, I'm a man without clothes, without a job," he murmured. "If you turn me away, I'm going to look might funny, hitchhiking back to Maryvale."

The vision made her lips lift slightly. "I bet you'd get picked up—half the town is women."

With a soft smile he asked, "How's the book coming?"

"Quite well—at least my editor says it is."

"I have an idea for a follow-up for you," he offered.

"You do?" she replied stunned.

He nodded. "There's a lighthouse on the Greek coast, purported to have seven dancing ghosts. Your next book could be about international lighthouse phantoms."

She cast him a dubious look. "Where did you hear such a thing?"

His shrug was sheepish and piercingly sweet. "I'm a stodgy scholar. Remember?"

She stepped away from him, scanning his near-naked form. "I don't know. You don't look particularly stodgy at the moment."

He lifted a querying eyebrow. "No?"

She shook her head.

"What do I look like?" he asked with a slow, devilish grin that sent tiny electrically charged thrills down the tender skin of her neck.

Rubbing her nape, she couldn't help but smile back. "You look like a crazy person standing there in your underwear."

He frowned in mock affront. "I came a long way just for an insult." The fringes of his dark lashes narrowed, as though he had a thought. "What if I weren't wearing them? How would I look?"

A purely wanton warmth invaded her belly as her mind's eye envisioned this magnificent man naked. She felt excited and alarmed all at once. What was happening? "I—don't know..." she managed, worried about what they might be unleashing here.

"Let's find out," he suggested, slipping off his Jockey shorts and flinging them on the flames. "What do I look like now?"

Her body went warm and weak. The crazy game was moving along too rapidly, and she was worried at how suddenly things had turned around. It couldn't be this easy. Dragging her gaze to his face, she asked, "This isn't a trick. I couldn't take it. Do you really mean it? We don't go back to AEI unless I want to?"

His lean face grew serious again. "Gina, I ask only two things of you."

"What?" She stiffened, expecting the worst.

He stepped close to her, taking her into his arms and whispering, "Burn that damned book you ordered and that infernal electrician's tape?" His tender kiss on her earlobe lasted only an instant before he released her.

She stared. It wasn't bright to melt this way, to trust him so quickly. He could bring disaster to her life so rapidly, and with so few words. But this time, something told her he really meant what he was saying.

"Will you do those two things for me?" he asked, his voice deep, almost reverent.

Reading the truth in his earnest expression, tears came to her eyes. He meant every word he said. Her lips trembling, she whispered, "I'll go get them."

When she turned to go, she felt a gentle tug on her wrist, "It'll keep, darling. Right now, we have some love to make."

Drawing her into his arms, he kissed her deeply. And Gina knew that whatever they decided to do, theirs would never be a dull alliance. If they did return to AEI—and she had a feeling they would—then that place, too, would be far from the stuffy institution she'd left behind. And this time, she would have her place there—a proud place by David's side.

When her naked husband lifted her into his arms, he murmured, "If we go up to the lighthouse, will I be stepping on any other man's toes?"

She curled her arms about his neck and smiled at him through her tears. "If you mean Paul, the last I heard, he and Iduna were licking their wounds together."

He chuckled. "Sounds kinky—but I'm happy for them." He carried her away from where the late Dean smoldered, toward the butter-colored squares of light that emanated from their cozy lighthouse.

"I'm eating salads now," she felt obliged to say, as she drifted along in his arms.

"Not right now, you're not," he warned suggestively. "You're going to be too busy to eat for a while."

A giggle bubbled in her throat. "I thought that would make you happy."

He halted, regarding her with a soft, heart-stopping gaze. "Darling, you have no idea how happy I am."

Their lips came together, and they savored the taste of this, their first kiss, for it was a first. Their lives, from this moment on, would never be the same. They were embarking upon a relationship in which a man and a woman not only loved equally, but sacrificed equally. Gina thought of her parents and David's, and knew a moment of sadness for the dominated women—and for their men, for they had never known the thrill and pride of accomplishments their wives might have made.

David lifted his lips from hers and murmured, "I brought you a box of chocolates."

Her mood lightened and she laughed, hugging him harder. A wild new thrill at being alive filled her as her husband began to walk with her again, toward their lighthouse. "I love you, David," she heard herself murmur. "But, if you don't mind, I think I'll have that wonderful, fattening, cholesterol-loaded box of chocolates bronzed."

Relishing the richness of his laughter, she rested her head against his sturdy shoulder as she sailed away to a harboring, exciting paradise that would serve them to the end of their days—a paradise that *she* had helped create.

my VALENTINE 1992

Celebrate the most romantic day of the year with
MY VALENTINE 1992—a sexy new collection of four
romantic stories written by our famous Temptation
authors:

> GINA WILKINS
> KRISTINE ROLOFSON
> JOANN ROSS
> VICKI LEWIS THOMPSON

My Valentine 1992—an exquisite escape into a romantic
and sensuous world.

 Harlequin Books®

HARLEQUIN *Temptation* ®

Rebels & Rogues

All men are not created equal. Some are rough around the edges. Tough-minded but tenderhearted. Incredibly sexy. The tempting fulfillment of every woman's fantasy.

When it's time to fight for what they believe in, to win that special woman, our Rebels and Rogues are heroes at heart.

Matt: A hard man to forget . . . and an even harder man not to love.

THE HOOD by *Carin Rafferty.*
Temptation #381, February 1992.

Cameron: He came on a mission from light-years away. . . then a flesh-and-blood female changed everything.

THE OUTSIDER by *Barbara Delinsky.*
Temptation #385, March 1992.

At Temptation, 1992 is the Year of Rebels and Rogues. Look for twelve exciting stories, one each month, about bold and courageous men.

Don't miss upcoming books by your favorite authors, including Candace Schuler, JoAnn Ross and Janice Kaiser.

HARLEQUIN'S "BIG WIN"
SWEEPSTAKES RULES & REGULATIONS
NO PURCHASE NECESSARY TO ENTER OR RECEIVE A PRIZE

1. Alternate means of entry: Print your name and address on a 3" x 5" piece of plain paper and send to the appropriate address below:

In the U.S.	In Canada
Harlequin's "BIG WIN" Sweepstakes	Harlequin's "BIG WIN" Sweepstakes
P.O. Box 1867	P.O. Box 609
3010 Walden Ave.	Fort Erie, Ontario
Buffalo, NY 14269-1867	L2A 5X3

2. To enter the Sweepstakes and join the Reader Service, scratch off the metallic strips on all of your BIG WIN tickets #1-#6. This will reveal the values for each Sweepstakes entry number, the number of free books you will receive and your free bonus gift as part of our Reader Service. If you do not wish to take advantage of our Reader Service but wish to enter the Sweepstakes only, scratch off the metallic strips on your BIG WIN tickets #1-#4. Return your entire sheet of tickets intact. Incomplete and/or inaccurate entries are ineligible for that section or sections of prizes. Torstar Corp. and its affiliates are not responsible for mutilated or unreadable entries or inadvertent printing errors. Mechanically reproduced entries are null and void.

3. Whether you take advantage of this offer or not, on or about April 30, 1992, at the offices of D. L. Blair, Inc., Blair, NE, your Sweepstakes numbers will be compared against the list of winning numbers generated at random by the computer. However, prizes will only be awarded to individuals who have entered the Sweepstakes. In the event that all prizes are not claimed, a random drawing will be held from all qualified entries received from March 30, 1990 to March 31, 1992, to award all unclaimed prizes. All cash prizes (Grand to Sixth) will be mailed to the winners and are payable by check in U.S. funds. Seventh Prize will be shipped to winners via third-class mail. These prizes are in addition to any free, surprise or mystery gifts that might be offered. Versions of this Sweepstakes with different prizes of approximate equal value may appear at retail outlets or in other mailings by Torstar Corp. and its affiliates.

4. Prizes: (1) ★ Grand Prize $1,000,000.00 Annuity; (1)First Prize $25,000.00; (1)Second Prize $10,000.00; (5)Third Prize $5,000.00; (10)Fourth Prize $1,000.00; (100)Fifth Prize $250.00; (2,500)Sixth Prize $10.00; (6,000) ★ ★ Seventh Prize $12.95 ARV.

   ★ This presentation offers a Grand Prize of a $1,000,000.00 annuity. Winner will receive $33,333.33 a year for 30 years without interest totalling $1,000,000.00.

   ★ ★ Seventh Prize: A fully illustrated hardcover book published by Torstar Corp. Approximate Retail Value of the book is $12.95.

   Entrants may cancel the Reader Service at any time without cost or obligation (see details in Center Insert Card).

5. This Sweepstakes is being conducted under the supervision of D. L. Blair, Inc. By entering this Sweepstakes, each entrant accepts and agrees to be bound by these rules and the decisions of the judges, which shall be final and binding. Odds of winning in the random drawing are dependent upon the number of entries received. Taxes, if any, are the sole responsibility of the winners. Prizes are nontransferable. All entries must be received at the address on the detachable Business Reply Card and must be postmarked no later than 12:00 MIDNIGHT on March 31, 1992. The drawing for all unclaimed Sweepstakes prizes will take place on May 30, 1992, at 12:00 NOON, at the offices of D. L. Blair, Inc., Blair, NE.

6. This offer is open to residents of the U.S., the United Kingdom, France, Germany and Canada, 18 years or older, except employees and immediate family members of Torstar Corp., its affiliates, subsidiaries, and all the other agencies, entities and persons connected with the use, marketing or conduct of this Sweepstakes. All Federal, State, Provincial, Municipal and local laws apply. Void wherever prohibited or restricted by law. Any litigation within the Province of Quebec respecting the conduct and awarding of a prize in this publicity contest must be submitted to the Régie des loteries et courses du Québec.

7. Winners will be notified by mail and may be required to execute an affidavit of eligibility and release, which must be returned within 14 days after notification or an alternate winner will be selected. Canadian winners will be required to correctly answer an arithmetical, skill-testing question administered by mail, which must be returned within a limited time. Winners consent to the use of their name, photograph and/or likeness for advertising and publicity in conjunction with this and similar promotions without additional compensation.

8. For a list of our major prize winners, send a stamped, self-addressed ENVELOPE to: WINNERS LIST, P.O. Box 4510, Blair, NE 68009. Winners Lists will be supplied after the May 30, 1992 drawing date.

Offer limited to one per household.

BWH192